G. J. STEIN

Daughter of Earth and Fire

First edition

ISBN: 979-8-9953294-0-4

This book was professionally typeset on Reedsy.
Find out more at reedsy.com

The world does not answer
desire.
It answers what is held long
enough to matter.

Contents

Chapter 1: The Fallen Cleric

In the heart of the verdant realm of Verahald where rivers ran like polished silver beneath the sun and ancient forests murmured secrets older than any kingdom — there lived a young human woman named Astrid.

She knelt at the edge of a stone fountain in the Temple Quarter of Eldoria, her reflection wavering in the water. Her hair, a fiery tumble of red curls, spilled loose down her back, catching the light like embers. Freckles dusted her pale skin, most noticeable now that worry had drawn the color from her cheeks. Around her neck hung a simple copper torque engraved with wheat and curling vines, the sacred symbol of Demetra, goddess of fertility, growth, and renewal.

Astrid pressed her palms together, whispering a prayer she had spoken a thousand times before.

"Lady of the Living Earth," she murmured, "hear me."

For a moment, nothing happened.

Then magic stirred.

It rose not as the warm, gentle tide she had known since

childhood, but as something erratic — flickering, biting, alive in all the wrong ways. The water in the fountain trembled. A spark of green-gold light flared between her hands, then sputtered violently.

Astrid gasped and pulled back just as the magic collapsed, leaving only cold stone and silence behind.

She bowed her head.

So it was again.

Astrid was — had been — a cleric of Demetra. A healer sworn to preserve life, to comfort the sick, to bless the harvests that fed the realm. Once, her touch could knit flesh and bone, soothe fever, coax flowers from barren soil. Once, Demetra's power flowed through her as naturally as breath.

Now it came and went like a storm that obeyed no season.

Behind her, the temple bells rang — a sharp, hollow sound that echoed through the white-stone streets of Eldoria. Astrid flinched. The bells no longer called her to service. They marked the hours she was no longer permitted to keep.

She rose slowly and turned away from the fountain, her shoulders squared despite the twisting ache in her chest.

The city unfolded around her in familiar splendor.

Eldoria was a crossroads of the civilized world: graceful elven spires rose beside human towers; dwarven stonework supported gnomish clockworks; halfling markets bustled beneath banners of every color. The air smelled of incense, fresh bread, and steel. Laughter and argument wove together into the living heartbeat of the city.

Astrid had once belonged here.

Now, as she walked through the crowds, she felt eyes on her — some curious, some wary, a few sharp with judgment. Whispers followed in her wake.

Chapter 1: The Fallen Cleric

"That's her…"

"The cleric who failed…"

"They say she nearly killed a man."

Astrid kept her gaze forward.

It had happened three weeks earlier — a simple healing spell cast on a wounded guardsman. The magic had surged wildly, burning instead of mending. Others had intervened before lasting harm was done, but the damage could not be undone where faith was concerned.

Unstable magic was dangerous magic.

The High Priestess had spoken kindly, but firmly. Astrid remembered every word.

Until this affliction is understood, you may not serve Demetra's altar.

They had taken her vestments. Her place. Her purpose.

She had walked out of the temple with nothing but the clothes on her back and the copper torque they had allowed her to keep out of mercy.

A sudden dizziness swept over her.

Astrid staggered, clutching the side of a vendor's stall as the world tilted. The sounds of the city blurred into a distant roar. Magic flared in her veins, untamed and sharp, like lightning beneath her skin.

"No," she whispered. "Not here."

Her knees buckled.

A shadow fell over her — a vast, sudden darkness that blocked the sun.

Strong hands caught her before she could hit the ground.

Carefully, impossibly gently, someone steadied her.

When Astrid lifted her head, she found herself staring into the chest of a giant.

Well — not a giant exactly.

A half-giant.

He loomed at least eight feet tall, his broad frame wrapped in dark leather and steel. His skin held the deep gray-blue hue of storm clouds at dusk, marked with faint scars that spoke of battle long past. Thick silver hair was bound at the nape of his neck, and his golden eyes regarded her with concern rather than alarm.

"Are you alright, little one?" he rumbled, his voice low and steady, like thunder far out at sea.

Astrid swallowed and nodded, forcing her breath to slow. "Yes. I think so. Thank you."

He didn't release her at once, waiting until she was fully steady before stepping back. Even then, he positioned himself between her and the flow of the crowd, a living wall of quiet protection.

"I felt the magic spike," he said. "It wasn't… gentle."

"That would be an accurate assessment," Astrid replied wryly.

Despite herself, she straightened. "I am Astrid. Cleric of Demetra."

Something passed behind his eyes — recognition, perhaps.

"Was," she amended softly.

The half-giant inclined his head. "Thorne Stoneward. Guardian of Eldoria. And protector of anyone who needs it."

Astrid hesitated, then asked, "You're not afraid?"

"Of a woman who nearly falls over in the street?" Thorne's lips twitched. "Terrifying."

She laughed softly before she could stop herself. It felt strange — foreign — but welcome.

Encouraged, Astrid told him everything. The failing magic. The whispers. The temple's judgment. As she spoke, the knot in her chest loosened, the weight shared at last.

When she finished, Thorne was silent for several breaths.

"I know a place," he said at last. "Far from the city. Older than the temples. The Oracle of the Whispering Woods."

Astrid's heart skipped. "The Oracle is real?"

"As real as you or I. And wiser than either." He studied her. "She speaks to the old gods — to the land itself. If answers exist, she will know them."

Hope flared — bright, dangerous.

"I will go," Astrid said without hesitation.

Thorne's brow furrowed. "The way is not safe."

"I was cast out," she said simply. "I have nothing left to lose."

For a moment, something fierce flashed across his face.

"Then you won't go alone."

They left Eldoria at dawn.

Beyond the city walls, Verahald revealed itself in unrestrained glory. Forests thick with emerald leaves stretched to the horizon. Pixies flitted between branches, trailing laughter and starlight. Ancient trolls guarded river crossings, their moss-covered forms as patient as the stones they resembled. Dwarven banners snapped in the thin mountain air as they ventured into higher ground.

Each day tested Astrid in new ways.

Her magic surged unpredictably — sometimes fading entirely, sometimes flaring too fiercely. Yet, paradoxically, her prayers to Demetra felt closer here, away from marble halls and formal altars. She spoke to the earth as she walked, fingers brushing leaves and bark, whispering gratitude for every living thing that thrived beneath the goddess's care.

Thorne watched her quietly.

At night, they shared stories by the fire. Astrid spoke of the temple gardens she once tended. Thorne spoke of standing watch on the city walls, of battles fought and friends lost.

One evening, by a stream that sang softly over smooth stones, Thorne handed her a cup of steaming tea.

"Drink," he said. "It will help you rest."

Their fingers brushed.

Magic sparked — not wild this time, but warm, steady, resonant.

Astrid looked up. Thorne froze, his breath shallow, eyes dark with something unspoken.

"I didn't mean — " she began.

"I know," he said gently. "But perhaps... it means something all the same."

Silence stretched between them, fragile and charged.

"You are stronger than you believe," Thorne said quietly. "Whatever this curse is — it does not define you."

Astrid swallowed hard. No one had said that to her. Not since the day she was cast out.

As the fire crackled and the stars wheeled overhead, hope took root once more — slow, fragile, but alive.

The road ahead was uncertain. The Oracle might condemn her as the temple had. Demetra herself might turn away.

Yet Astrid no longer walked alone.

And somewhere deep within Verahald's living heart, the goddess watched, patient as the seasons, waiting for the fallen cleric to find her way home.

Chapter 2: The Whispering Woods

The journey to the Whispering Woods was a test of Astrid's resolve, but with Thorne by her side, she found an unexpected source of strength. The half-giant's presence was a comforting anchor in the storm of her uncertain magic, and his quiet support gave her the courage to face each new challenge.

As they ventured deeper into the wilderness, the landscape grew wild and untamed. The trees twisted into gnarled shapes, their branches intertwining to form a dense canopy that filtered the sunlight into dappled shadows. The air was thick with the scent of earth and growing things, and the sounds of the forest were a symphony of life — birdsong, the rustle of leaves, and the distant knock of a woodpecker.

Astrid felt a strange sensation as they entered the Whispering Woods. It was as if the very air was alive with magic, pulsating with an energy that resonated deep within her soul. Her steps became lighter, and her heart swelled with a sense of belonging she hadn't felt since her exile from the temple. The surges came less often now, but when they did, they felt denser — coiled power rather than chaos.

Thorne noticed the change in her demeanor and raised an eyebrow. "You seem different," he rumbled, his voice a soft rumble that blended with the forest sounds.

Astrid smiled, her eyes shining with a newfound vitality. "I feel different. This place... it's alive. I can feel Demetra's presence here, stronger than ever before."

Thorne nodded, a small smile playing at the corners of his mouth. "The Whispering Woods are ancient, sacred ground. Many come here to seek the Oracle's wisdom, but few are granted an audience. You are fortunate, Astrid."

Thorne had not walked Eldoria's walls in years. His oath went where it was needed, not where it was comfortable — a truth evident in how naturally he moved through places older than any city.

Astrid's smile faded as she thought of the trials that lay ahead. "Fortunate, perhaps, but also fearful. What if the Oracle cannot help me? What if my magic is beyond redemption?"

Thorne placed a large, reassuring hand on her shoulder. "Do not let doubt cloud your mind. You have come this far, and you have faced your fears with bravery. The Oracle will see that. Have faith, Astrid."

His touch was warm and comforting, and Astrid found herself leaning into it, drawing strength from his presence. She took a deep breath and nodded, determined to face whatever lay ahead with the same courage that had seen her through the journey so far.

As they delved deeper into the woods, the path grew more treacherous. Roots snaked across the ground, and rocks jutted out like teeth, but Thorne's sure footing and Astrid's newfound determination saw them through. They crossed a bubbling stream, its water clear and cold, and climbed a steep hill, their breaths coming in ragged gasps by the time they reached the top.

At the summit, they found a clearing, and in the center stood a massive tree, its trunk twisted and gnarled with age. Its leaves shimmered in iridescent hues, and a soft glow emanated from within, casting an ethereal light on the surrounding area. Astrid's eyes widened in awe as she approached, feeling the pulsating magic that seemed to radiate from the very heart of the tree.

"This is it," Thorne said, his voice a hushed whisper. "The Oracle resides within."

Astrid reached out a tentative hand, her fingers brushing against the bark. A jolt of energy coursed through her, and she gasped, stepping back. The tree seemed to hum with life, and she could almost hear the whispers of the ancient magic that dwelled within.

"I am Astrid," she said, her voice steady despite the tremor in her heart. "Cleric of Demetra. I seek the Oracle's wisdom."

For a moment, nothing happened. Then, slowly, the tree began to change. The bark shifted and shimmered, taking on the appearance of flesh and skin. The face of an ancient woman emerged from the trunk, her eyes wise and knowing, her expression serene.

"Greetings, child," the Oracle said, her voice like the rustling of leaves. "You are not Astrid."

Astrid's heart skipped a beat, and she exchanged a confused glance with Thorne. "I… I am Astrid," she stammered. "Cleric of Demetra."

The Oracle's gaze bore into her, unyielding. "You seek me out, yet you do not know your true name. Say it aloud, and I will grant you audience."

Astrid's mind raced, but she could not fathom what the Oracle meant. She looked to Thorne for support, and he gave her an encouraging nod. Taking a deep breath, she closed her eyes and reached within, searching for the truth of her identity.

"Lady of the Living Earth," she whispered, "guide me to my true self."

A shiver ran through her, and when she opened her eyes, she knew. "I am Astrid, Daughter of the Earth, Chosen of Demetra."

The Oracle's expression softened, and she nodded. "Welcome, Daughter of the Earth. I have been expecting you."

Astrid's heart leaped with hope. "You know why I am here?"

The Oracle nodded, her gaze shifting to Thorne. "And you have brought a worthy protector. Good. The path ahead will not be easy, Astrid. Your magic is indeed cursed, but it is also a gift — a gift that can be honed and controlled."

Astrid's eyes filled with tears of relief. "How? Please, tell me how to break this curse."

The Oracle's expression turned somber. "The cure for your ailment lies within the heart of the mountains, where the ancient dragons reside. Seek the Dragon's Tearstone, a gem of pure magic, and with it, you may purify your powers. But be warned, the journey will be perilous, and you will face trials that will test the very limits of your strength and resolve."

Thorne stepped forward, his voice steady and sure. "We will face whatever comes our way. Astrid is not alone in this quest."

The Oracle smiled, a gentle curve of her lips that held an eternity of wisdom. "Then go, with my blessings. May the ancient magic of this forest guide and protect you both."

Astrid and Thorne bowed their heads in gratitude, and as they turned to leave, the Oracle called out to them one last time. "Remember, Astrid — your magic is a reflection of your inner self. To control it, you must first understand yourself. The

Dragon's Tearstone will show you the way. But know this — the gem is not merely a cure; it is a choice. Choose wisely, for the fate of your magic, and perhaps even your soul, depends on it."

With those final words echoing in their minds, Astrid and Thorne set off on the next leg of their journey, their hearts filled with renewed hope and determination. The Whispering Woods seemed to sigh around them, the whispers of the ancient magic a soft, encouraging murmur as they ventured forth into the unknown, ready to face the trials that awaited them in the dragon's lair.

Chapter 3: The Dragon's Lair

As Astrid and Thorne journeyed deeper into the heart of the mountains, the landscape grew more treacherous. The air thinned, and the winds howled through the craggy peaks, carrying with them a sense of ancient power and danger. Astrid clung to Thorne's massive frame, her small hands gripping the fur at his neck as he carried her through the snow-covered passes. His silver hair flowed behind him like a banner, and his broad shoulders bore the weight of their journey with unyielding strength.

Astrid couldn't help but steal glances at Thorne, her eyes tracing the contours of his face — his strong jaw, the scar that ran across his cheek, and the gold flecks in his eyes that seemed to glow with an inner fire. He was a tower of strength and comfort, a beacon of hope in the harsh, unforgiving wilderness. His presence gave her the courage to face the trials ahead, and she found herself drawn to him in a way she hadn't expected.

"Thorne," she called out, her voice barely audible over the howling wind. "Tell me about yourself. I want to know more about you."

Thorne looked down at her, his expression softening. "What would you like to know, Astrid?"

"Everything," she replied, a small smile playing at the corners of her mouth. "How did you become a guardian? What is your life like in Eldoria? Do you have family?"

Thorne was silent for a moment, as if weighing his words. "I was not always a guardian. I was a warrior in the service of the king, fighting in battles and skirmishes across the realm. But I grew weary of war and the senseless killing. I sought something more — something with purpose. That's when I became a guardian, sworn to protect the innocent and uphold justice."

He paused, his grip tightening around her as they navigated a particularly treacherous stretch of ice. "As for Eldoria, it is a city of contrasts — grand and majestic, yet fraught with poverty and strife. I have a small dwelling near the city walls, humble but sufficient for my needs. And family? I had a sister, but she passed away many years ago. She was taken by an illness that even the most skilled healers could not cure."

Astrid's heart ached for him, and she reached up to squeeze his arm in sympathy. "I'm sorry, Thorne. That must have been very difficult for you."

Thorne nodded, his voice barely a rumble. "It was. But I honor her memory by living a life of service and protection. That is what gives me purpose now."

Astrid felt a deep sense of admiration and respect for Thorne. His dedication and selflessness were qualities she aspired to emulate. She leaned against him, finding comfort in his warmth and strength.

As they continued their ascent, the snow gave way to bare

rock, and the wind died down, leaving an eerie silence in its wake. The air grew warmer, and a faint, sulfurous smell tinged the otherwise crisp mountain air. Astrid's heart pounded in her chest as she realized they were approaching the dragon's lair.

Thorne set her down gently, his eyes scanning the surroundings with a keen gaze. "We are close, Astrid. Stay alert and follow my lead."

Astrid nodded, her hand resting on the pommel of her sword. She took a deep breath, steeling herself for what lay ahead. The entrance to the lair was a yawning chasm in the side of the mountain, shrouded in shadows and mist. As they stepped inside, the air grew hotter, and the stench of sulfur and something far more primal and dangerous filled their nostrils.

The walls of the cavern were lined with glistening crystals that cast an ethereal glow, illuminating the path ahead. Astrid's steps echoed ominously as they ventured deeper into the heart of the mountain. The dragon's presence was palpable, a throbbing pulse of power that seemed to vibrate through the very stone beneath their feet.

Suddenly, Thorne stopped, his hand shooting out to bar Astrid's path. "Listen," he whispered, his voice barely audible.

Astrid held her breath, straining her ears. At first, she heard nothing but the distant drip of water and the rumble of the mountain. Then, slowly, she began to make out a rhythmic, deep breathing — a sound that sent shivers down her spine.

Thorne's hand dropped, and he drew his sword, the blade gleaming in the crystal light. "Stay close to me, Astrid. Whatever happens, do not leave my side."

Astrid nodded, her heart hammering in her chest as she gripped her own weapon, her knuckles white with tension.

They rounded a bend, and there it was — the dragon, coiled in the heart of the cavern, its scales shimmering like a lake of liquid gold. Its eyes, ancient and wise, regarded them with a mix of curiosity and annoyance.

Astrid's breath hitched as she beheld the magnificent creature. She had heard tales of dragons, but nothing could have prepared her for the awe-inspiring sight before her. The dragon's body was massive, its muscles rippling beneath its scales, and its wings, folded neatly against its back, were unlike anything she had ever seen.

Thorne stepped forward, his voice steady and clear. "Greetings, mighty dragon. We seek an audience with you, for we have need of your wisdom and power."

The dragon's eyes narrowed, and it let out a low rumble that echoed through the cavern. "What brings a half-giant and a cleric to my lair, seeking wisdom and power? Speak quickly, for I grow weary of your presence."

Astrid took a deep breath, her voice steady despite the fear that gripped her heart. "I am Astrid, Daughter of the Earth, Chosen of Demetra. I seek the Dragon's Tearstone, a gem of pure magic, to purify my corrupted powers and restore balance to my life. Will you aid us in our quest?"

The dragon's gaze shifted to Astrid, and she felt as if she were being stripped bare, her very soul laid bare before the ancient beast. After what felt like an eternity, the dragon spoke, its voice like the rumble of distant thunder.

"I will aid you, Astrid, but first, you must prove yourself worthy. Your magic is unstable, and you have shown little control over it. I sense a deep well of power within you, but it is chaotic and wild. To wield the Dragon's Tearstone, you must first master your own abilities."

Astrid's heart sank, but she met the dragon's gaze unflinchingly. "What must I do?"

The dragon's eyes gleamed with a challenge. "I will grant you a single task. Heal the heart of this mountain. It has been wounded by the dark magic that plagues these lands, and it suffers. If you can restore it to health, I will grant you passage to the Dragon's Tearstone."

Astrid glanced at Thorne, who nodded encouragingly. She turned back to the dragon, determination in her eyes. "I will do it."

The dragon nodded slowly. "Very well. Approach the crystal formation at the far end of the cavern. There, you will find the source of the mountain's ailment. Purify it, and you will have proven your worth."

Astrid took a deep breath and made her way to the crystal formation, her steps echoing through the cavern. As she approached, she could feel the pulsating darkness emanating from the crystals, a malevolent force that seemed to twist and writhe like a living thing.

She reached out a tentative hand, her fingers hovering just above the crystals. Magic surged within her, wild and untamed, but she focused her intent, channeling her power into the crystals. The darkness resisted, pushing back against her efforts, and suddenly, the crystals began to glow with an eerie red light. The mountain shuddered, and Astrid felt a wave of dread wash over her. She feared that she was harming the mountain rather than healing it.

"Demetra, guide me," she whispered, her voice trembling with effort and desperation. For a moment, she doubted that her goddess would hear her, that her prayers would fall on deaf ears. But she pressed on, pouring her strength into the crystals, her breath coming in ragged gasps as she fought to purge the darkness.

Suddenly, a searing pain shot through her, and she cried out, staggering back. Her hand was covered in blood, and the crystals glittered with a sinister energy. She had failed.

Thorne rushed to her side, his arm supporting her as she slumped against him. "Astrid, are you alright?"

She nodded weakly, her voice barely a whisper. "I... I tried. But it was too strong."

The dragon observed them, its expression unreadable. "Your effort was commendable, Astrid. But you have shown that you are not yet ready to wield the Dragon's Tearstone. You must return and train, hone your skills, and gain control over your magic. Only then will you be worthy of the gem's power."

Astrid's heart ached with disappointment, but she knew the dragon was right. She had underestimated the task and paid the price. "I understand," she said, her voice steady despite the turmoil within her. "I will return, and I will prove myself worthy."

The dragon's eyes held a flicker of disappointment, but also a spark of hope. "You came close, Astrid. The mountain responded to your touch, but your control is lacking. Return when you are ready, and I will grant you another chance."

With those final words echoing in their minds, Astrid and Thorne bowed their heads in gratitude, ready to embark on the next leg of their journey. The dragon's lair seemed to sigh around them, the whispers of ancient magic a soft, encouraging murmur as they prepared to face the trials that awaited them. Astrid felt a pang of unease, a sense that the true challenges of her quest were only just beginning. Yet, with Thorne by her side and the dragon's wisdom guiding her, she faced the unknown with a steadfast heart, ready to embrace whatever lay ahead in the heart of the dragon's domain, knowing that she had to return and train harder to gain control over her magic and prove herself worthy of the Dragon's Tearstone.

Chapter 4: The Space Between Flame and Stone

The mountain gave them no resistance when they left.

No tremor followed their steps. No rumble of displeasure echoed after the dragon's voice faded into memory. The cavern's heat cooled with unsettling speed, stone reclaiming its dominion as if Astrid had never touched it at all.

That silence hurt more than the pain in her hand.

Astrid kept her injured palm close to her chest as Thorne guided her through the winding paths back toward the open air. He did not rush her. He did not speak. His presence — vast and steady — was the only thing keeping her upright as the weight of her failure settled fully into her bones.

When at last the cavern mouth spilled them into cold mountain air, Astrid broke.

Her knees buckled, and she would have fallen if Thorne had not caught her, one massive arm sweeping her up with practiced ease. The sudden closeness stole her breath — not from surprise, but from how naturally she fit against him, wrapped in strength that asked nothing of her in return.

"I should walk," Astrid murmured, though she made no move to pull away.

Thorne ignored the protest. "You will," he said calmly. "Later."

He carried her until they reached a sheltered ledge carved into the mountainside, where jagged stone curved inward to block the worst of the wind. Firelight soon flickered against the rock as Thorne coaxed flame from flint, the small blaze a humble thing compared to the powers they had faced — but real, and warm.

Astrid sat where he placed her, staring down at her blood-stained hand.

"I almost hurt it," she whispered. "The mountain."

Thorne crouched in front of her, impossibly large even at rest, silver hair falling loose around his shoulders. He took her wrist gently, turning her palm upward to inspect the wound. His touch was careful, reverent even.

"You stopped," he said. "That matters."

"Too late."

"No." His voice was firm now. "Before you broke it further. Before you broke yourself."

Astrid let out a shaky breath. "I prayed," she admitted. "And for a moment, I thought she didn't hear me. Demetra. I thought... maybe she was done with me."

Thorne met her gaze, eyes steady, unflinching. "Faith is not tested when answers are easy."

She laughed weakly. "You sound like a cleric."

"My sister was one," he said. "Before she died."

Astrid stilled. He had spoken of her before — but rarely with such softness.

"She used to say that the gods do not abandon us," Thorne continued. "They step back, so we must learn to stand."

Astrid closed her eyes. "I don't know how."

"You learn," he said simply. "Like everyone else."

He wrapped her injured hand carefully, using a strip torn from his own cloak. His fingers brushed her skin, warm and grounding, anchoring her in the present when her thoughts threatened to spiral.

For the first time since leaving the dragon's lair, Astrid allowed herself to cry — but quietly, silently — tears slipping down her cheeks without sound. She did not hide from him. And Thorne did not tell her to be strong.

He stayed.

When the tears passed, Astrid felt hollow but calmer, like land after a storm.

"I've been relying on will," she said after a long while. "Force. I thought if I pushed hard enough, believed fiercely enough, the magic would obey."

"And now?" Thorne asked.

"And now I think I've been trying to command something that wants partnership." She looked at her wrapped hand. "I don't listen to it. I just demand."

Thorne considered her words thoughtfully. "I fought like that once," he said. "Tried to overwhelm every threat through strength alone. It worked — until it didn't."

"What changed?"

"I broke," he said evenly. "And in the breaking, I learned restraint."

Astrid looked up at him. "You never seem restrained."

A faint smile touched his mouth. "Appearances deceive."

Chapter 4: The Space Between Flame and Stone

The fire crackled between them, embers drifting upward like fading stars. Astrid found herself watching the rise and fall of his chest, the way his armor sat loosely on a body shaped by battles he rarely spoke of. She wondered — not for the first time — how someone so powerful could carry such quiet patience.

"You don't look at me like I'm dangerous," she said suddenly.

Thorne met her gaze. "You are dangerous."

She swallowed.

"But danger," he continued, "is not the same thing as harm."

Something in his words settled deep within her, easing a tightness she had carried since exile.

They made camp there for the night.

Astrid dreamed restlessly — of roots cracking stone, of fire blooming in her veins — but when she woke, dawn painted the mountains in soft gold instead of blood-red flame.

For the first time, she did not reach for her magic.

She listened.

They spent the morning moving slowly along the mountain's lower paths, Astrid forcing herself to feel each step, each breath. When frustration rose — and it did — Thorne did not correct her. He simply waited.

It was infuriating.

And revelatory.

By midday, Astrid realized something unsettling.

Without magic, she was still here.

She noticed the world more clearly — the way wind shaped snowdrifts, how stone carried heat longer than it should, how her heartbeat no longer raced at every quiet moment. The absence of power did not make her lesser. It made her present.

That frightened her more than failure ever had.

That night, as Thorne adjusted the fire, Astrid spoke into the dark.

"When I return to the dragon," she said, "I think he'll refuse me again."

"Possibly."

"And if he does?"

Thorne looked at her then, truly looked at her. "Then you will keep growing. And when you are ready — he will know."

"And you?" she asked quietly. "Will you still be with me when I fail again?"

There was no hesitation in his answer. "Yes."

The certainty in his voice sparked something low and dangerous inside her — not heat, not yet, but a pull she did not try to name.

Astrid nodded once, holding his gaze.

"Then I will learn," she said. "Not to conquer my magic. To understand it."

Thorne smiled — a rare, unguarded thing. "That," he said, "is how you survive dragons."

As the fire burned low, Astrid found herself leaning against him, her head resting lightly against his arm. He did not move away.

And for the first time since exile, Astrid slept without fear.

Chapter 5: Lessons Written in Stone

Astrid woke before dawn.

The fire had burned down to embers, the mountain air sharp against her skin. For a moment, she lay still, disoriented — then memory settled in like a second weight. The dragon's denial. The failure. The ache in her hand, now tightly bound and sore.

And Thorne.

She turned her head carefully.

He slept on one knee a short distance away, massive form half-turned toward her even at rest, as if vigilance were instinct rather than choice. His silver hair had slipped loose during the night, pale strands catching the faint glow of dying coals. Without armor, without movement, he looked carved from the stone itself — quiet power contained.

He seemed even larger like this — broader somehow — his weight settled into the stone as if the mountain itself had accepted him. One thick arm rested loose across his knee, veins faint beneath scarred skin, hands made for weapons and walls and breaking things, now utterly still.

Astrid looked away quickly, heat flickering beneath her ribs — not magic, she told herself sharply. Just awareness. Just foolishness born of exhaustion.

She had never known safety to look like this. Never known power to be quiet.

Astrid looked away before she could think too long on that.

She rose slowly, wincing as stiffness pulled at her muscles, and wrapped her cloak tighter around herself. The world felt different this morning. Not lighter, exactly — but sharper, more defined. Every sound carried farther. Every sensation lingered.

She closed her eyes and reached inward, carefully — as one might touch a bruise to test its tenderness.

Magic stirred.

Not violently. Not eagerly.

It waited.

Astrid let out a slow breath. She did not push. She did not command.

She opened her eyes again.

"You're awake early."

Thorne's voice was low, roughened by sleep. He was watching her now, golden eyes alert even as he rose in a single smooth motion.

"I didn't mean to wake you," Astrid said.

"You didn't."

There was something unreadable in his expression — approval, perhaps.

Breakfast was simple. Dried fruit, hard bread warmed by the fire. They ate mostly in silence, the mountains blushing pink as the sun crept higher.

After a while, Astrid spoke. "I need to learn."

Thorne waited.

"Not spells," she clarified. "Not new ones. Control. Listening. Whatever it is I keep doing wrong."

"You're asking me to teach you magic," Thorne said gently.

"No." She met his gaze. "I'm asking you to help me create space to learn."

That earned her a faint smile.

"I can do that."

They moved farther down the mountain, to a shelf of stone overlooking a narrow ravine where meltwater carved its patient path through rock. Thorne stopped there, surveying the area, then nodded once.

"This will do."

Astrid frowned. "For what?"

"For failing," he said calmly. "Safely."

He gestured to the ravine. "Stone deep enough to absorb backlash. Water to ground excess energy. And room to retreat."

Astrid swallowed. "You've done this before."

"Enough."

She stepped away from him, heart hammering — not with fear alone, but anticipation. Not heat, exactly. Focus.

She raised her uninjured hand, palm open toward the stone wall across the ravine.

"Don't aim," Thorne said.

She hesitated. "But — "

"Don't shape," he continued. "Just listen."

Astrid closed her eyes.

The magic was there — coiled, compressed, pressing against

her ribs like breath held too long. Her instinct screamed to *release* it, to push it outward and be done with it.

She didn't.

She listened instead — to the rhythm beneath it. The slow patience of stone. The steady insistence of water. The weight of the world simply being what it was.

Her magic wavered.

Then surged.

Sharp pain lanced up her arm as energy snapped out of control, exploding into the ravine in a flash of green-gold light. Stone cracked. Water hissed.

Astrid cried out and staggered back —

— and ran straight into Thorne.

His hands caught her shoulders, firm and unyielding, grounding her instantly. Heat radiated from him, solid and undeniable.

"Breathe," he said.

She did, panicked and shallow at first, then deeper as his grip steadied her.

"I can't," she gasped. "It still feels like it wants to tear free."

"It will," Thorne said. "For a while."

His thumbs shifted, just slightly, pressing into muscle and bone. Astrid became acutely aware of how close they were — of how small her hands felt against his chest, of how steady his breathing was compared to hers.

"You're not broken," he continued. "You're learning the cost of restraint."

Something in her chest tightened.

"I don't like failing."

"No one does."

"I don't like how it feels when I lose control."

Thorne's voice dropped. "Neither do I."

There was more in that than he said. Astrid didn't ask. Not yet.

They practiced until her arms shook and her head throbbed. Sometimes the magic answered in hesitant trickles. Sometimes it lashed out wildly. Each time, Thorne adjusted — moving closer or farther away, saying nothing unless she asked.

He never touched her unless she lost balance.

Which happened more than once.

By late afternoon, Astrid collapsed onto a sun-warmed boulder, exhausted beyond anything she had felt before. Sweat clung to her skin beneath her clothes. Her magic lay quiet — not gone, but spent.

Thorne crouched nearby. "That's enough for today."

She let out a breath that was almost a laugh. "You don't sound disappointed."

"I'm not."

She turned her head to look at him. "I failed. Repeatedly."

"And you're still standing," he said. "That's progress."

Astrid smiled faintly. Then, before she could stop herself, she reached out and rested her head briefly against his arm.

He did not pull away.

For a moment, neither of them spoke.

The sun dipped lower, casting fire across stone. Astrid felt something stir — not magic this time, but awareness. Of him. Of herself. Of how the space between them felt... charged and fragile all at once.

Thorne shifted first, standing and offering her a hand.

She took it.

As his fingers closed around hers — careful, restrained — Astrid thought that perhaps this, too, was a kind of training.

Learning when not to reach.

Chapter 6: When Stone Pushes Back

Astrid failed before sunrise.

The magic didn't wait this time. It struck sharp and sudden, bursting loose as she reached for the river's edge, sending a spray of dirt and shattered stone skittering across the ravine floor.

She reeled back with a curse, heart pounding, breath ragged.

Thorne moved instantly — between her and the backlash, body set, stance wide — but the magic had already spent itself. Silence followed, heavy and accusing.

Astrid squeezed her eyes shut.

"I was listening," she said. "I didn't push. I didn't *try*."

Thorne studied the scorched stone where roots had been moments before. Then he looked at her.

"I know."

"That's worse," she snapped.

The words left her mouth before she could temper them. Fatigue sharpened everything — edges too close, nerves too bare.

Thorne did not react. He waited.

Astrid dragged a hand through her hair, pacing. "Yesterday I could feel it. The rhythm. The patience. Today it's like it's fighting me."

"Learning isn't a straight line," Thorne said.

She whirled on him. "Easy for you to say."

The instant the words landed, shame followed.

"I didn't mean — "

"You did," he said calmly. "And you're allowed to."

That only made her chest tighter.

They moved higher into the foothills as the morning wore on, searching for terrain that felt… right. Nothing did. The land resisted her touch — too dense, too sharp, too *aware*.

By midday, her magic lashed unpredictably, sparks snapping where she tried to coax calm.

Each failure dug deeper.

"I was chosen," Astrid said suddenly, voice shaking. "Demetra knew me. Trusted me."

Thorne turned to face her fully.

"And you think that trust disappears because you struggle?"

"I think maybe I mistook obedience for faith."

The admission scraped its way out of her chest.

Thorne was quiet for a long moment. "Faith that is never questioned is not faith," he said finally. "It's habit."

Astrid let out a harsh breath. "Then I'm terrified of what's underneath mine."

They stopped near a sheer rock face streaked with mineral veins — gold and green running through gray stone like frozen lightning. Thorne surveyed it, then nodded once.

"Here," he said. "This stone remembers pressure."

Astrid stepped up to it hesitantly. She placed her palm

against the cool surface — careful of her injured hand — and breathed.

The magic rose slowly.

She tried to open herself to it. Tried to *listen*.

The stone pulsed.

Then *pushed*.

Pain lanced through her arm as the magic recoiled violently, throwing her backward. Astrid cried out as her heel slipped on loose gravel —

— and suddenly Thorne was there, hands catching her waist, momentum slamming her flush against his chest.

Too close.

Her breath stalled.

His hands were firm, certain, fingers spread across her back, anchoring her instantly. She could feel the steady rhythm of his heartbeat beneath her ear — solid, grounding, unyielding.

"Stay," he said, low and urgent.

Her magic stilled.

Not vanished. Not defeated.

Contained.

Astrid didn't move. Neither did he.

She became acutely aware of everything — the heat of his body against hers, the way her palms rested uselessly against his chest, the way his breath brushed the crown of her head.

"This is dangerous," she whispered — not about the magic.

Thorne's grip tightened fractionally. "I know."

He did not release her immediately. And she did not ask him to.

For one suspended moment, the world narrowed to stone and breath and the hum of something neither of them named.

Then Thorne stepped back, deliberately, distance restored

like a wall hastily raised.

Astrid swayed slightly, steadying herself. Her cheeks burned.

"That wasn't failure," Thorne said.

"It felt like it."

"No," he replied. "That was resistance. — Yours. The land's. And mine."

She lifted her gaze. "Yours?"

Thorne looked away, jaw tight. "You're not the only one trying to relearn restraint."

The admission landed quietly — and heavily.

Afternoon passed in strained attempts. Small successes flickered, then vanished. Control remained elusive.

By evening, frustration gnawed at Astrid's resolve. When she finally sank down against a boulder, exhausted and shaking, tears burned behind her eyes.

"I don't know how to do this," she said hoarsely. "I don't know if I can."

Thorne knelt in front of her, massive presence steady, unyielding.

"You can," he said. "But not alone."

She laughed weakly. "You keep saying that."

"Because you keep believing you have to suffer through this by yourself."

She finally looked at him then — really looked at him. At the scars he carried. The restraint he wielded like armor.

"How do *you* endure it?" she asked softly. "Holding yourself back all the time?"

Thorne met her gaze. "Some days, I don't."

The honesty in his voice stole her breath.

Night settled thick and quiet around them. They made camp without speaking much, exhaustion dulling sharp edges.

Later, wrapped in cloak and firelight, Astrid stared up at the stars.

"I'm afraid," she said quietly.

Thorne shifted closer — close enough that warmth seeped through her cloak, but not touching.

"I know," he said.

"But I'm still here."

His gaze found hers through the dark. "So am I."

That was all.

It was enough.

Astrid closed her eyes, exhaustion finally claiming her. And though the magic still coiled restlessly beneath her skin, she slept — knowing now that resistance was not punishment, but invitation.

Chapter 7: What Almost Breaks

The hills were restless that night.

Astrid felt it long before the magic responded — an unease in the land, a tension threaded beneath stone and root. Even the fire seemed uncertain, flames rising and falling as if caught between decisions.

She sat close to its warmth, knees drawn up, absently flexing her injured hand. The ache had dulled, but it never fully faded. A reminder. A warning.

Across from her, Thorne sharpened a blade in slow, careful strokes. The faint rasp of stone against metal filled the quiet, rhythmic and steady.

"You don't need to keep watch tonight," Astrid said softly. "Nothing's come near us for days."

Thorne didn't look up. "That's usually when it does."

She smiled faintly. "You can't guard against everything."

That finally earned her his attention. Golden eyes lifted to hers, unreadable.

"I try anyway."

The honesty in his voice tugged at something inside her — something sharp and tender all at once.

Astrid looked back at the fire. “Earlier,” she said, choosing her words slowly, “when the magic surged… it wasn’t anger this time.”

Thorne set the blade aside. “What was it?”

She exhaled. “Longing.”

The word lingered between them.

“For what?” he asked.

“I don’t know,” she admitted. “Belonging. Release. Understanding. Maybe all of it.” Her fingers curled into the fabric of her cloak. “It’s worse when I’m… distracted.”

Thorne’s jaw tightened. “Then we’ll adjust.”

“By distancing?”

“By awareness,” he corrected. “Distance doesn’t always help.”

She glanced at him. “You sound like you’ve learned that lesson the hard way.”

Something flickered behind his eyes — old, controlled, dangerous.

“Yes,” he said simply.

Silence stretched again, heavier now. The kind that pressed instead of soothed.

Astrid stood abruptly. “I should practice. While it feels like this.”

Thorne rose at once. “At night?”

“It doesn’t wait for daylight,” she replied.

They moved beyond the fire’s reach to a bare shelf of stone, moonlight painting the world in silver and shadow. The air felt charged — alive.

Astrid planted her feet, grounded herself, and lifted her hands.

The magic responded instantly.

Not violently. Not gently.

Eager.

She stiffened. "That's new."

Thorne circled her slowly, watchful. "What does it feel like?"

"Like it's…" She faltered, searching for the word. "Aware. Of everything."

She reached deeper — not to command, but to open herself, to listen.

Something shifted.

The land answered with a low hum, vibration passing through stone into bone. Astrid gasped as the magic surged — hot and compressed, coiling tight behind her ribs.

"Thorne — " she whispered.

"I've got you," he said, already there.

His hands settled on her arms — not restraining, just present. The contact sent a shock through her that had nothing to do with magic.

The surge faltered.

Then spiked.

Light flared around them, green-gold and volatile. Astrid cried out as the ground beneath her feet cracked, energy scrambling for release.

"Focus on me," Thorne said, voice low and urgent. "Not the magic. Me."

She looked up into his eyes — and everything else fell away.

The magic shuddered.

"It's reacting to you," she breathed. "To us."

Thorne swallowed. "Then don't let it decide for you."

Her hands trembled. His grip tightened — not to control, but to anchor.

Their faces were close. Too close.

Astrid became acutely aware of how his breath brushed her cheek. How warm his hands were against her skin. How easily she could lean forward that final inch.

"This is a mistake," she whispered.

"Yes," Thorne agreed.

Neither moved.

The magic coiled tighter, pressure building, responding to the space *not* closing between them.

Astrid's heart thundered. "If we don't — "

"I know."

His forehead dipped slightly, nearly touching hers.

The world narrowed to breath and stone and fire burning low behind them.

Astrid's lips parted.

Thorne stopped breathing.

The magic snapped.

A violent pulse exploded outward, throwing them apart as the land rejected the strain. Stone fractured with a sharp crack, light blinding and sudden, magic lashing like a living thing freed too quickly.

Astrid screamed as pain ripped through her arms, the backlash slamming her to the ground.

"ASTRID!"

Thorne was moving before the echo faded, at her side in an instant. He hauled her upright, shielding her from another surge as the magic dispersed into the night with a thunderous sigh.

Silence followed. Heavy. Broken only by Astrid's harsh breathing.

She clutched at Thorne's chest, fingers digging into leather, disoriented.

“I’m sorry,” she gasped. “I didn’t mean — ”

He gathered her close, arms wrapped fully around her now, no restraint left in the gesture. She felt his heart racing, his breath uneven.

“I know,” he said hoarsely. “I should’ve stepped back.”

“No,” she protested weakly. “I shouldn’t have — ”

“Enough.” He loosened his grip just enough to look at her, hands still firm at her waist. “This isn’t blame.”

Her eyes burned. “Then what is it?”

Thorne hesitated.

“The truth,” he said at last. “Your magic reacts when you deny what you feel. Not when you feel it — but when you refuse to acknowledge it.”

Astrid froze.

“You’re saying — ”

“I’m saying restraint without honesty is just another kind of control,” he finished quietly.

The words hit harder than the backlash.

Slowly, Thorne released her and stepped away. Distance returned — not easily, but deliberately.

“We can’t do that again,” he said, voice steady but strained. “Not like that.”

Astrid’s chest ached. “Because of the danger?”

He met her gaze. “Because neither of us will stop next time.”

The admission stole her breath more surely than any magic.

They returned to camp in silence, the night suddenly colder.

Later, wrapped in her cloak, Astrid stared at the remnants of the fire.

Her magic was quiet now — but not calm.

She understood something she hadn’t before.

This wasn't just about learning control.

It was about learning truth.

Behind her, Thorne settled at the edge of the firelight, posture rigid, eyes fixed somewhere far beyond the hills.

Neither slept easily.

Between them lay the space of almost — a promise deferred, a danger named, and a bond neither magic nor fear could undo.

The land remembered.

So did they.

Chapter 8: The Weight of What Wasn't

Morning came quietly.

Too quietly.

Astrid woke with the uneasy sense that something vital had been misplaced — not lost, exactly, but set down somewhere she could not reach. The fire had burned low again, little more than a scatter of embers pressed into ash. The hills lay still beneath a pale sky, stone washed clean by dawn's thin light.

She sat up slowly, every muscle protesting.

Thorne was already awake.

He stood a short distance away, back turned, armor half-fastened as he tightened a strap across his chest with deliberate care. He did not look toward her as she shifted beneath her cloak. Did not acknowledge her presence until the metal finally settled into place with a soft, final click.

"You should eat," he said, voice steady and neutral. "Before training."

Chapter 8: The Weight of What Wasn't

Training.

The word landed with dull finality.

Astrid nodded, though he could not see it. She accepted the bread and dried fruit he set beside the fire, fingers brushing only ash where his warmth had been moments before. They ate in silence, the space between them too carefully maintained, as if closeness itself had been marked dangerous.

Astrid tried not to think about how easily their breathing had aligned the night before.

How the land itself had responded.

That was the problem, she realized. Avoidance did not erase memory. It sharpened it.

They moved away from camp after breakfast, descending into a shallow valley where the stone softened and soil gave grudging way to life. Sparse grass clung to cracks in the earth. Pale flowers bowed their heads to the morning wind.

"This ground is thinner," Thorne said. "Less resistant. It may answer you more easily."

Or fall apart faster, Astrid thought — but she kept that to herself.

She stepped forward and closed her eyes, centering herself as she'd been shown. Breath first. Then listening. The magic stirred obediently at the edge of her awareness — a coiled presence, waiting to be acknowledged.

She acknowledged it.

The earth hummed faintly beneath her bare feet.

A stone lifted from the ground, no larger than her palm. For a heartbeat, it hovered — steady, calm.

Astrid exhaled slowly.

Then the magic shuddered, pressure rising abruptly, coiling tighter, searching.

Astrid snapped her eyes open and broke contact at once. The stone dropped harmlessly back into the dirt.

Control.

Not mastery. Not release.

Progress.

She glanced toward Thorne, uncertain whether to claim the small victory.

He had not been watching her.

His attention was fixed on the ridge above them, gaze sharp, posture alert, every inch the guardian once more. The distance stung more than she expected. She swallowed and turned away, grounding herself again.

They practiced like that for hours — Astrid testing small movements of power, stopping before strain could escalate; Thorne acting as silent barrier rather than anchor, never touching, never closing the space.

It was harder than facing backlash.

By midday, the strain had settled deep into Astrid's bones. Sweat clung to her hairline. Her injured hand throbbed, tension radiating up her arm.

She broke first.

"Are you avoiding me?" she asked.

The question echoed in the open air between them — exposed, impossible to take back.

Thorne turned slowly.

"No," he said after a moment.

Astrid folded her arms tightly, unsure whether that made her relieved or wounded. "Then why won't you look at me?"

Something tightened in his expression — jaw set, eyes narrowing just a fraction.

"Because if I do," he said carefully, "I won't be thinking about training."

The honesty bit deeper than reproach ever could.

Astrid's breath caught. "Thorne — "

"This isn't punishment," he continued. "And it isn't distance. It's… discipline."

Her mouth curved in a humorless smile. "You're very good at that."

"Yes," he said evenly. "That's why I know when it's failing."

The admission sat heavy between them.

Astrid dropped her arms, suddenly very tired. "I don't want to feel like a danger to you."

"You're not," Thorne replied instantly. Then, more quietly, "You're a danger to yourself when you deny what you feel."

Astrid turned away before he could see the heat that flared behind her eyes — not magic, not entirely. Something more fragile.

They traveled again that afternoon, pushing deeper into unsettled terrain. The land grew steeper, stone rising in jagged lines that caught the light like broken glass. Astrid found herself growing more cautious — not just with her magic, but with her thoughts.

Every time her awareness drifted toward Thorne — his size, his steadiness, the way his presence had once anchored her — her power stirred restlessly in response.

The connection terrified her.

By evening, clouds had gathered low along the horizon, bruised with the promise of storm. Wind curled through the pass, carrying the scent of rain and iron.

"We should shelter," Thorne said. "Soon."

They found it in a narrow cleft between two outcroppings — stone worn smooth by centuries of weather. The space forced them closer than either had allowed all day.

Astrid felt it immediately.

Her breath slowed unnaturally. The magic within her stirred, prickling along her skin, drawn to the shared warmth, the enclosed space, the proximity she had tried so hard to ignore.

She pressed her back to cold rock, grounding herself through sensation alone.

Thorne crouched near the entrance, broad form blocking the worst of the wind. He moved deliberately, as though aware that careless motion could tip something precarious.

The storm broke shortly after dusk.

Rain battered the stone above them, sharp and relentless. Twilight deepened into shadowed gray, the world reduced to sound and closeness and breath. Thorne tended the small fire, movements efficient, restrained.

Astrid watched him from the corner of her vision, heart too loud in her chest.

She hated this — hated the distance layered over closeness, hated the way effort was now required not to reach. Worse, she hated that the magic listened when she slipped.

A crack of thunder rolled across the pass.

Astrid flinched despite herself.

Thorne's head snapped up. Without thinking, he reached out a hand toward her — then stopped, fingers hovering inches from her shoulder.

They both went still.

The magic surged in response — tight, compressed, pressing for release.

Astrid swallowed hard. "It's reacting again."

"I know," Thorne said quietly.

She took a shaky breath. "I didn't do anything."

"No," he agreed. "You didn't."

The realization sank in like cold water.

"This isn't just about control, is it?" she whispered.

"No."

Thorne lowered his hand slowly, placing it against the stone instead, knuckles whitening as he braced himself. "It's about honesty. And choice."

Astrid nodded, heart aching with unsaid things.

Outside, rain lashed the rocks. Inside, the space between them felt dangerously alive.

Later, when the storm had dulled to steady drizzle, exhaustion finally claimed them both. They slept in the small shelter — back to wall, not touching, distance measured carefully.

Astrid dreamed of roots winding through stone. Of fire burning low but steady. Of a hand reaching — and stopping.

When morning came, the land smelled clean and sharp, washed by rain.

Astrid woke with resolve sharp in her chest.

She would learn this. Not just control. Not just magic.

Truth.

And the courage to face what the land already knew.

✦✦✦

They camped where the stone broke unevenly into long, sloping shelves, the earth softened just enough with wind-blown loam to make sitting possible without sinking. Twilight came slow here, light thinning rather than falling away, the world narrowing to muted color and breath.

Astrid felt the day in her bones.

Not pain — fatigue of a quieter kind. The kind that made

awareness sharper rather than duller. Her magic lay still beneath her skin, contained but alert, like a held exhale. She had learned to recognize that state now.

Thorne noticed her stillness.

"You're holding," he said quietly, not accusation — observation.

She nodded. "It's easier than letting it drift right now."

He considered that, then reached into his pack and retrieved a small flask. "Then drink first. Before your attention turns inward."

She accepted it. Their fingers brushed.

Not accidentally.

Astrid's breath caught — a small, treacherous thing. The contact was brief, barely there, but it landed with disproportionate force, awareness flaring sharp and sudden along her nerves.

The magic stirred.

Not violently.

Attentively.

Astrid closed her fingers around the flask and pulled her hand back before it could escalate. She took a careful sip, grounding herself through the taste of cold water and mineral.

Thorne sat across from her, one knee bent, forearms resting loosely there. He hadn't moved closer — but he hadn't drawn away either.

The space between them felt… articulate.

"This is the hardest part," she said suddenly.

Thorne looked up. "Which part?"

"Knowing when proximity is support," she said, choosing her words carefully, "and when it becomes something else."

His gaze held hers, steady and unflinching. "And which do

you think this is?"

Astrid hesitated.

The truth pressed behind her ribs — not dangerous, just frightening in how easily it named itself.

"I think," she said softly, "it could be either. Depending on what I do with it."

He nodded once. "That sounds right."

The fire crackled between them — low, controlled. Astrid found herself watching the light slide across the plane of his forearm, the scar there pale against darker skin. She wondered — not for the first time — how often restraint had been mistaken for absence in his life.

"May I?" Thorne asked quietly.

She didn't ask what he meant.

"Yes," she said.

He shifted closer — deliberately slow, giving her time to refuse. When he placed his hand at her wrist, it was gentle but sure, fingers warm, thumb settling against the pulse there.

Astrid froze.

The magic reacted instantly — tightening, coiling, drawing closer to the surface like something curious rather than alarmed.

She breathed.

"Still with me?" Thorne murmured.

"Yes," she said. "Don't stop."

He didn't increase pressure. Didn't pull her closer. His touch remained exactly what it was — present, anchoring, restrained with surgical precision.

Astrid became acutely aware of everything: the heat of his palm, the steadiness of his breathing, the fact that she could remove her wrist at any moment — and did not.

Want pooled low in her chest, sharp and undeniable.

She let herself feel it.

The magic wavered... then settled.

"Oh," she breathed.

"What?" Thorne asked.

"It isn't spiking," she said, awe threading her voice. "It's... listening."

His thumb shifted slightly, barely a movement, but the intimacy of it sent a shiver through her. "And you?"

She swallowed. "I am painfully aware of you."

A pause.

Thorne's voice lowered. "So am I."

The air between them thickened, weighted not with urgency but intention. Astrid felt herself lean forward on instinct — and stopped.

Her heart hammered. Desire surged hotter, sharper —

— and she held.

"This is the line," she said quietly.

"Yes," Thorne agreed. He didn't move. Didn't release her either. "Do you want to cross it?"

Astrid searched her own reactions — not for fear, but for honesty.

"No," she said. And then, because truth mattered: "Not like this."

Relief and disappointment tangled, sharp but clean.

Thorne nodded. His hand loosened — not abruptly, not retreating — but easing away with care, as if unhooking something fragile rather than rejecting it. When his fingers left her skin, Astrid felt the absence keenly — and noted, with quiet triumph, that the magic remained calm.

They sat there for a long moment, breathing settling, the

world resuming its ordinary sounds.

"I wanted to," Astrid admitted eventually.

Thorne's mouth curved faintly. "I know."

"And you didn't..."

"I won't decide timing for you," he said gently. "Or for us."

She met his gaze. Something solid formed there — not promise, not caution. Understanding.

"That mattered," she said.

"Yes," he agreed. "It did."

They shifted then — slightly apart, but not distant. The fire burned low. The night continued.

Astrid pressed her palm briefly to the earth, grounding herself through habit rather than need. The land did not react.

She smiled.

The wanting hadn't been denied.

It had been **chosen to wait**.

Chapter 9: The Land Does Not Stay Silent

Astrid sensed it before she saw it.

The air grew taut, as if stretched too thin between breaths. Stone beneath her boots hummed faintly — not the deep patience she had learned to recognize, but something sharper, restless. The magic within her stirred in response, not surging, but pressing outward, alert and uneasy.

She slowed, hand lifting instinctively.

"Thorne," she said quietly.

He stopped at once, already turning, gaze sweeping the ridge above them. "Yes."

Something moved.

A ripple passed through the ground ahead — soil shifting, pebbles skating loose across stone. The sparse grass along the slope bent sharply, roots tearing free as the earth itself recoiled.

Astrid's heart lurched. "That's not — "

Chapter 9: The Land Does Not Stay Silent

The ground convulsed.

Stone burst upward in a jagged spray as a creature hauled itself free — long — limbed and angular, formed of rock and root and something darker threaded through the cracks. Its shape twisted unnaturally, shards grinding together as it rose, hollow pits where eyes should have been glowing faintly red.

A corrupted earth — wraith.

Astrid staggered back. "I didn't summon that."

"No," Thorne said grimly, already moving in front of her. "But it felt you."

The wraith let out a sound like grinding stone, shoulders hunching as it lurched toward them, drawn by the pressure of Astrid's magic like hunger made manifest.

Astrid swallowed hard. "This is my fault."

"This is a consequence," Thorne corrected. "Different thing."

The creature surged forward, claws tearing into stone. Thorne stepped to meet it without hesitation, blade flashing as it struck. Steel rang against rock, sparks flaring as the wraith recoiled with a furious shriek.

Astrid's pulse thundered. Her magic coiled tight, begging for release.

She planted her feet, forcing herself to breathe.

No wild power. No panic.

The wraith pivoted suddenly, bypassing Thorne with unnerving speed, its hollow gaze fixed squarely on Astrid.

Thorne swore under his breath. "Astrid — move!"

She did, stumbling sideways as the creature's claw slammed into the ground where she'd stood moments before, stone splintering violently.

The magic in her chest surged in response — hot, compressed, furious at the threat.

Astrid raised both hands.

"Listen," she whispered — whether to the magic or the land, she did not know.

The earth shuddered.

Not violently this time — but deliberately.

Stone beneath the wraith's feet softened, turning pliable as wet clay. The creature shrieked, losing purchase as the ground began to swallow it.

The pressure was immense.

Astrid screamed as pain lanced up her arms, magic straining dangerously close to rupture. Her knees buckled —

— and suddenly Thorne was there.

His arm wrapped around her waist, hauling her back against him, his other hand braced against the ground, anchoring them both as if sheer will could steady stone.

"Not everything at once," he growled into her ear. "Guide it. Don't fight it."

Astrid clung to his arm, breath sobbing, desperately trying to *shape* instead of force.

The earth responded.

The wraith sank deeper, stone hardening around it deliberately now — roots winding tight, holding, containing. With a final wrenching cry, the creature was dragged fully beneath the surface, ground sealing over it with a low, resonant thud.

Silence fell abruptly.

Astrid collapsed fully this time, every muscle shaking as the magic drained away, leaving her hollow and trembling.

Thorne caught her before she hit the ground, lowering them both carefully to one knee. His grip was firm, protective, arms enclosing her without hesitation now.

She buried her face against his chest, breath ragged. "I didn't mean to draw it. I swear."

"I know," Thorne said, voice rough with something she'd never heard there before. "That's what frightens me."

Her head snapped up. "Me too."

For a long moment, neither moved.

Astrid became keenly aware of how tightly he held her — how his heart hammered beneath his armor, how his breath was anything but steady. The magic within her remained quiet now, spent and watchful.

"That thing," she said slowly. "It wasn't attacking the land. It was responding to me."

"Yes."

"And if there are more?"

"There will be," Thorne said honestly. "The farther we go. The more unsettled your magic remains."

Guilt clawed painfully at her chest. "You shouldn't have to face that."

Thorne's jaw tightened. "I choose what I face."

The words struck deeper than he likely intended.

Astrid pulled back slightly, just enough to look at him. "That doesn't mean I get to be reckless."

"No," he agreed. "It means we proceed differently."

She frowned. "How?"

Thorne hesitated, then released her slowly, rising to his feet and offering her a hand. She took it, unsteady but determined.

"You don't train alone anymore," he said. "Not when the land reacts this strongly."

Astrid's pulse picked up. "You mean you'll — "

"I mean proximity," he finished. "Controlled. Conscious. Together."

Her breath stalled.

"That's dangerous," she said.

"Yes," he replied evenly. "But so is pretending distance solves this."

The honesty left her dizzy.

They moved again shortly after, skirts of the hillside littered with cracked stone where the wraith had risen. Every step Astrid took felt weighted now — not with fear, but responsibility.

That night, they made camp beneath an overhang of red-veined rock. Thorne's presence stayed close — not touching, but unyielding in its nearness. Astrid felt the magic respond quietly, settled rather than strained.

She stared into the fire, mind racing.

"You didn't hesitate," she said at last. "When it came for me."

Thorne looked up, eyes reflecting flame. "Never."

The certainty in his voice sent heat coiling low in her chest — not magic this time, not entirely.

Astrid lowered her gaze, heart pounding. "If this is what my magic does to the world when I'm not honest — "

"Then honesty becomes part of control," Thorne said gently.

She swallowed. "Even when it's inconvenient."

"Especially then."

They sat in silence after that, the weight of what lay ahead settling heavy but real.

Astrid understood something vital now: The land would not wait for her comfort. Neither would desire. Neither would consequence.

Control would not come from denying any of it.

She closed her eyes, resolve forming like bedrock beneath her ribs.

Tomorrow, she would try again. Not alone. Not unaware.

And the land, watching closely, would decide what answered back.

Chapter 10: What the Earth Asks in Return

Astrid did not sleep.

She lay awake long after the fire had burned equal parts coal and memory, staring into the dark beneath the stone overhang while rainwater dripped steadily somewhere beyond reach. Each drop sounded too loud. Too deliberate. Like punctuation she had not earned.

Every time she closed her eyes, she saw stone tearing open. Felt the lurch of the earth as it gave birth to something twisted and wrong — all because she had passed through it carrying power she could not yet contain.

I did that, she thought.

Not intentionally. Not maliciously.

But still.

Her magic lay quiet beneath her skin, coiled tight and watchful, as if it, too, waited to see what choice she would make next.

Chapter 10: What the Earth Asks in Return

Eventually, when the night had thinned into something gray and formless, Astrid sat up and drew her cloak around herself. The ground beneath her felt different now — not hostile, but aware in a way that prickled along her spine.

Thorne was already awake.

He stood near the edge of the shelter, facing outward, one massive arm braced against the stone. He did not turn when she shifted, but his presence registered immediately — steady, unyielding, as constant as gravity.

"You should rest," he said quietly.

Astrid exhaled. "I don't deserve to."

Thorne turned then, slowly, as if meeting her gaze required thought.

"That's not how this works."

She hugged her knees to her chest. "That creature yesterday — if it had reached the lowlands, hurt someone — "

"It didn't," he said.

"But it *could have.*" Her voice tightened. "And if I keep going like this, something worse will answer eventually."

Thorne crossed the small space between them, crouching so his eyes were level with hers. He did not touch her — not yet.

"You're assuming responsibility means isolation," he said.

Astrid swallowed. "It means *regulation.* Control. Caution."

"Yes," he agreed. "And also honesty. Planning. Accountability." His gaze sharpened. "Not punishment."

The word struck deeper than she expected.

"I don't know how to hold power like this," she admitted. "And I don't know how to forgive myself when it spills over."

Thorne considered her for a long moment. Then he did something unexpected.

He sat.

Not beside her. Not in front of her as guardian. But across from her, legs folded awkwardly beneath his weight, armor creaking faintly.

"When my sister fell ill," he said without preamble, "I broke protocol. I left my post. I took her beyond the city walls, sought healers I wasn't authorized to consult. I defied direct orders."

Astrid's heart twisted. "Because you loved her."

"Yes." His jaw tightened. "And because I believed my strength could compensate for limitation. That if I pushed hard enough — fought hard enough — I could bend the world into giving me a different outcome."

He met her gaze evenly. "I was wrong."

Astrid felt that truth settle in her bones.

"She died anyway," Thorne continued. "And the consequences of my choices did not vanish with her. Innocent people were left unguarded that night. One paid the price."

Astrid's breath caught. "Thorne — "

"I tell you this because guilt untreated becomes something dangerous," he said. "It either rots inward, or it demands reckless redemption."

She closed her eyes, hands trembling. "What am I supposed to do, then? Pretend it doesn't matter?"

"No," he said firmly. "You're supposed to let it matter **without letting it control you**."

Silence stretched between them, thick and honest.

Astrid pressed her palm flat against the ground, grounding herself through sensation alone. The earth felt cool. Solid. Present.

"What if responsibility means choosing limits?" she asked quietly. "What if it means I don't use magic at all, unless there's no other choice?"

Thorne tilted his head slightly. "That's restraint."

"And restraint is good."

"Yes."

"But you keep saying restraint alone isn't enough."

His voice lowered. "Because responsibility is not just about what you refrain from doing. It's about what you prepare for."

Astrid frowned. "Meaning?"

He leaned forward slightly — not crowding, but intentional. "If your magic draws attention, you don't pretend it won't. You plan for it. You don't avoid proximity because it feels dangerous — you manage it because it *is*."

Her pulse skipped.

"You mean — "

"I mean we train with safeguards," Thorne said. "Boundaries. Signals. Physical distance agreed upon, not improvised. You learn what your magic does in response to fear, desire, anger — not by suppressing those emotions, but by observing them safely."

Astrid's chest tightened. "Together."

"Yes."

The word felt heavier than magic.

She nodded slowly. "Then I need to accept that things will answer me."

"And that doesn't make you a threat," Thorne said. "It makes you powerful."

The distinction mattered more than she could express.

They spent the morning reshaping their approach.

Astrid marked a perimeter using simple stones — points of grounding she could retreat to if pressure became too great. Thorne positioned himself not as shield, but as anchor — close enough to feel, far enough not to provoke the surge they now understood too well.

She practiced small interactions: coaxing warmth into cold stone, encouraging moss to grow along a shaded crevice, lifting pebbles and letting them fall without force.

Each success was quiet. Earned.

Each failure was contained.

Still, the guilt lingered — not crushing, but persistent.

By afternoon, Astrid's movements had slowed, exhaustion settling deep into her limbs. She lowered herself onto the ground, back against a boulder, staring out across the uneven valley below.

"I don't want to be forgiven for this yet," she said quietly.

Thorne stood nearby, gaze sweeping the horizon before returning to her. "Why not?"

"Because I don't think I've earned it."

He was silent for a long moment. Then, carefully, he stepped closer — just close enough that she felt the warmth of him beside her without contact.

"Responsibility isn't waiting until you're perfect," he said. "It's showing up tomorrow anyway."

Astrid looked at him then — really looked at him. At the restraint etched into every line of his posture. At the weight he carried without demanding absolution.

Her throat tightened.

"I don't want my magic to hurt the world," she said. "Or you."

Thorne's voice was low and certain. "Then we make decisions that honor that."

"And if I fail again?"

"Then we adjust."

The simplicity of it nearly undid her.

As dusk crept down the valley, Astrid felt something shift — not in her magic, but in herself. The guilt no longer pressed her into the ground. It rooted her there instead.

Responsibility wasn't avoidance.

It was commitment.

That night, they sat near the fire — not touching, but close enough that the space between them felt chosen rather than imposed. Astrid rested her hands over the earth, feeling its steady presence beneath her palms.

For the first time, the land did not stir restlessly in response.

It waited.

So did desire.

And Astrid understood, with quiet certainty, that both were asking the same thing.

Not denial.

But care.

Chapter 11: The Shape of Shelter

The temperature dropped without warning.

Astrid felt it first in her hands — sensation draining too quickly from skin into bone, fingers stiffening despite movement. The air sharpened, breath turning thin and biting between one step and the next. The wind shifted sharply through the ravine, pouring cold down from the peaks above like spilled water searching for depth.

Storm coming, she thought.

Thorne halted mid-step, already lifting his gaze to the sky. The clouds above had thickened into a low, bruised mass heavy with snow rather than rain, their edges blurred and volatile.

"We need shelter," he said. "Now."

They found it barely in time.

The cave cut shallow into the mountainside — more a wound than a room — its stone walls slick with mineral veins that caught faint light and distorted it into dull, colorless glints. The space was narrow and low, forcing Astrid to duck instinctively as she entered.

Too small to stand comfortably.

Too small for distance.

She felt the awareness settle almost immediately — not panic, not alarm, but recognition. The way the body notes proximity before the mind assigns meaning.

Thorne moved first, efficient and economical, shrugging his pack free and setting to work coaxing fire from damp wood and flint. The flame took reluctantly, sputtering low and defensive against the cold rather than banishing it.

Astrid wrapped her cloak tighter around herself, teeth already beginning to chatter despite restraint.

"This isn't normal," she said quietly. "The cold."

Thorne nodded. "The storm's pulling heat straight out of the stone."

Her magic stirred instinctively at the threat — just a flicker, a tightening beneath her ribs — as if rising habit wanted to answer before consent had fully formed.

"No," Thorne said gently, already turning toward her. "Not yet. Let's see what's necessary first."

Astrid swallowed and nodded. Responsibility before reaction.

Minutes passed. The fire struggled. The wind harried the cave mouth relentlessly, curling cold fingers past stone and cloth alike. Astrid's hands tingled painfully now, stiffness creeping through wrists and forearms.

She pressed her palm quietly to the cave floor and listened.

The stone was too cold.

Too drained.

There was nothing to draw without forcing compensation elsewhere.

"I can't pull warmth from this," she said. "There's nothing to take without damaging the substrate."

Thorne considered that — briefly, fully — then removed his gauntlets and set them aside with deliberate calm.

"Then we conserve what we have."

Astrid looked up sharply. "What do you mean by — "

Body heat.

The understanding landed before the words did.

They both went still.

The cave seemed to tighten around them, not with danger, but inevitability.

"That's..." Astrid swallowed. Her breath fogged in the thinning air. "That's going to provoke a response."

"Yes," Thorne said evenly. "Which is why we do it intentionally. With boundaries."

Her heart hammered painfully in her chest — not from fear, but awareness sharpened by exhaustion and closeness and everything unspoken that lay between them.

"Controlled proximity," she said.

"Exactly."

She exhaled once, slow and steady. This wasn't indulgence. This was survival.

Thorne settled first, bracing himself against the far wall of the cave, knees bent to account for his size. He wrapped his cloak around his broad shoulders and extended one arm — open, offered, not pulling.

"Sit here," he said. "Back to my chest. We'll ground together."

Astrid hesitated only a breath.

She moved carefully, deliberately, lowering herself into the space he offered.

The moment her back met his chest, sensation flooded her.

Heat — solid and immediate — radiated into her spine

through layers of cloth and cloak, startling in its intensity. Thorne's body was unmoving behind her, an unyielding wall that neither pressed nor withdrew. His arm curved securely around her waist, firm without constriction, anchoring without possession.

Astrid sucked in a breath she hadn't realized she'd been holding.

The magic responded instantly — coiling, tightening, drawn by warmth and proximity like a living thing startled into consciousness. Not violent. Not chaotic.

Alert.

Her pulse spiked anyway.

"It's reacting," she whispered.

"I know," Thorne murmured near her ear. "Breathe. Acknowledge it. Don't suppress."

Astrid closed her eyes.

She focused on the rise and fall of his breathing instead of her own. Slow. Measured. Steady in a way nothing else had been for days.

The first inhale was too shallow. The second steadied. On the third, her magic shifted — not retreating, not surging, but settling like a blade being sheathed with care.

Relief loosened its grip on her chest.

This is possible, she thought.

And then — because truths refused to remain untested — awareness slid beneath that relief.

Thorne's chest rose against her back with each breath, and with it came the undeniable fact of him: his size, his heat, the immense strength held so carefully it felt deliberate rather than cautious. His forearm around her waist stayed exactly where it was. Not higher. Not lower. No wandering. No claim.

Only choice.

Astrid became painfully aware that choice could be changed.

Not by accident.

By decision.

Minutes passed. Time tilted. The fire dimmed to a steady glow, but his warmth did not waver. Astrid realized she was listening for more than the wind now — listening for herself.

The line between necessity and desire did not vanish.

It sharpened.

Thorne shifted slightly to block a fresh gust curling into the cave. The movement pressed her closer — not careless, not indulgent, simply practical.

Astrid gasped softly.

Instantly, his arm tightened a fraction — not possessive, not demanding, but grounding.

"Easy," he said quietly.

The magic stirred again — curious, attentive.

"I'm trying," she whispered. "It's harder when — "

"I know," he said.

His breath brushed her temple. "Name it."

Astrid's pulse hammered. "I'm aware of you."

A pause.

"So am I," Thorne said.

The honesty landed like heat where it had no business being, slow and deliberate.

Astrid pressed her palm flat to the stone beside her, grounding herself through sensation rather than force.

"This isn't loss of control," she said aloud, partly to convince herself. "This is awareness."

"Yes," Thorne agreed. "And awareness can be managed."

She tested that deliberately. She adjusted her weight just slightly back, enough to feel the boundary of his presence more clearly.

The magic hummed — tense but contained.

Thorne did not move.

Good.

The space between her shoulder and his throat felt impossibly small. Astrid could imagine turning her head, her mouth close enough that breath alone would change something irreversible.

She did not.

Stillness here was not avoidance.

It was discipline.

Thorne's hand remained steady at her waist — present, precise. He didn't tighten his hold or retreat from it.

He stayed.

Want pooled low inside her, sharp and undeniable. She acknowledged it without feeding it.

And the magic, astonishingly, settled further — as if it understood the difference between denial and pacing.

They stayed like that through the worst of the storm. When the wind softened and the cold eased, Astrid realized her fear had changed shape.

Not gone.

Transformed.

She turned her head just enough to look back.

Their faces were close — too close to pretend neutrality. Thorne's eyes were steady, intent, restraint etched into them like oath.

"We did it," she said softly.

Thorne nodded. "You did."

"And the magic held."

"Yes."

They didn't smile.

They didn't need to.

Eventually, Thorne loosened his hold slowly, giving her space without withdrawing altogether. Astrid stepped away, the absence of his heat sharp but manageable.

Their eyes met across the narrow cave.

Something unspoken passed between them — not promise, not regret.

Acknowledgment.

The storm passed fully sometime before dawn.

Astrid slept in shallow intervals, wrapped in exhaustion rather than fear. When she woke again, the mountains were pale with new snow and the air felt clean instead of knives-sharp.

Thorne was awake already, posture unchanged, gaze fixed outward.

"You should rest," he said quietly.

"I did," she replied — and realized it was true.

She pressed her palm briefly to the stone. The land felt calm.

Accepting.

She exhaled slowly.

Whatever lay ahead would not be simple.

But for the first time since leaving Eldoria, Astrid knew something with quiet certainty:

Desire did not negate discipline.

Closeness did not destroy control.

And shelter — when chosen carefully — could reshape more than stone.

Chapter 12: Things Said in the Open

The storm passed during the night, leaving the air thin and clean in its wake.

Astrid woke slowly, wrapped in the soft ache of exhaustion rather than pain. For a moment she lay still, letting sensation return piece by piece — the steady rise of her chest, the cool stone beneath her hand, the faint warmth lingering in the shelter where they had shared space not long ago.

Thorne was awake.

She could feel it before she saw him — a presence no longer guarded by distance, but by intention. He stood near the mouth of the cave, looking out over the valley, armor set aside, shoulders bare beneath the gray light of morning.

Astrid pushed herself upright, careful not to jostle her injured hand.

"We should talk," she said quietly.

Thorne stilled — but he did not turn away.

"Yes," he said. "We should."

They gathered their things in silence first. It felt important not to rush the words ahead of readiness, not to let them spill uncontrolled the way magic once had. The land outside was damp and still, faint mist clinging to low stone and sparse grass.

They moved down into the valley before stopping — far enough that the cave no longer pressed around them, but close enough that the memory of it lingered.

Astrid folded her arms, unsure where to begin. Her thoughts tangled easily now, emotion layered over awareness in ways she was still learning to untangle.

"Last night," she said finally, "wasn't an accident."

Thorne met her gaze at once. "No."

"And it wasn't just necessity."

"No."

The truth sat between them, solid as stone.

Astrid nodded. "I need to know something, before this goes any further."

Thorne waited.

"When you pull away — when you keep control so tightly — are you protecting me?" Her voice wavered only slightly. "Or yourself?"

For the first time since she had known him, Thorne hesitated not out of calculation, but vulnerability.

"Both," he admitted.

Astrid exhaled, relief and ache mingling. "Then at least we're being honest about that."

He gave a short, quiet huff of something like a laugh. "You always were relentless with truth."

"I'm trying to be," she replied. "The land doesn't forgive pretense. Neither does magic."

"Nor desire," Thorne added softly.

Her heart stuttered — but she didn't look away this time.

"I don't want to pretend this isn't there," she said. "And I don't want to... rush it into becoming something dangerous."

"I don't either," Thorne said. His voice was steady, but she could see the restraint carved into him like a second skin. "What I feel doesn't invalidate caution. And caution doesn't invalidate what I feel."

Astrid let the words settle.

"That's the part I keep struggling with," she admitted. "I was taught that if something threatens balance, it must be denied."

"And I was taught that if something threatens order, it must be restrained," Thorne said. "Neither lesson teaches how to live with what remains."

They stood there, side by side, the valley opening wide and quiet around them.

Astrid pressed her palm briefly to the earth, grounding herself through habit now rather than desperation. The land answered — not with pressure, but acknowledgment.

"What happened with the wraith," she said carefully, "made something very clear."

"That you're not the only one affected by your power," Thorne said.

"Yes. But also that avoidance doesn't prevent consequence." She met his gaze. "It just delays it."

Thorne nodded once. "That realization has buried more cities than wars."

She smiled faintly. "Comforting."

He returned it, small but genuine.

They resumed training later that morning, deliberately and slowly. Astrid practiced holding warmth without drawing more than the stone could spare, shaping small responses rather than grand gestures. Thorne stayed present — but not constant — allowing space, then returning deliberately when needed.

At one point, Astrid faltered — not from magic, but emotion. She sat back on her heels, breath unsteady.

"I don't want to mistake control for denial anymore," she said quietly. "And I don't want to mistake desire for recklessness."

Thorne knelt nearby, close enough to feel, far enough not to overwhelm.

"Then we name things as they are," he said. "Without acting on them until we choose to."

Astrid nodded. "Choice matters."

"Yes."

She studied him for a long moment — the scars, the strength, the restraint that had once felt immovable and now felt intentional.

"Tell me something, Thorne," she said.

"Anything."

"If the night had gone on longer — if the cold hadn't retreated — would you have stepped away?"

Thorne's jaw tightened. But he didn't deflect.

"No," he said. "I would have held you exactly as long as was needed."

Astrid swallowed.

"And after?" she pressed.

His gaze held hers. "After, I would have waited."

The answer struck deeper than passion would have.

They returned to camp that evening with something settled between them — not diminished tension, but grounded understanding. The fire burned steadily. The land felt calm.

As dusk bled across the stone, Astrid watched the way the

light caught in Thorne's silver hair, the way his presence no longer threatened to pull her magic from equilibrium.

"Thank you," she said suddenly.

"For what?"

"For not deciding for me," she replied. "For letting this be… shared."

Thorne inclined his head. "Power was never meant to be carried alone."

Night fell gently.

They sat close — not touching, but without the careful avoidance of before. Astrid felt the magic within her remain quiet, attentive but unperturbed.

Desire lingered.

So did restraint.

And for the first time, neither felt like an enemy of the other.

They felt like allies.

Chapter 13: The Line They Chose Not to Cross

The day unfolded slowly, as if the land itself had decided not to rush them.

Mist clung to the ravine well past sunrise, softening the jagged edges of stone into something gentler, almost forgiving. Astrid welcomed the pace. After the storm, after the admissions of the night before, anything hurried felt dangerous.

She spent the morning in quiet practice.

No theatrics. No reach for grandeur. Just warmth coaxed into cold stone until frost retreated a finger's width at a time. Just pebbles lifted and settled again, their brief hover measured by breath rather than effort.

Thorne did not interrupt.

He remained nearby — always nearby — but not watchful in the way he had been days ago. His attention drifted between horizon and ground, posture relaxed but weighted with thought. When he did glance at her, it was not with vigilance, but with something steadier.

Acknowledgment.

It unsettled her more than distance ever had.

By midday, Astrid's temples throbbed dully, exhaustion creeping in not from exertion, but restraint. She lowered herself onto a sun-warmed slab of rock, tilting her head back to let the light hit her face.

"I think," she said carefully, "that ignoring what I feel takes more energy than managing it."

Thorne's mouth curved slightly. "That's often true."

"But managing it requires… clarity."

"Yes."

"And honesty."

"Yes."

She glanced at him sideways. "That's the part I'm still afraid of."

He did not pretend otherwise. "So am I."

They didn't move closer. They didn't step away.

Instead, they let the words rest between them — an open truth rather than a challenge.

Later in the afternoon, Thorne suggested relocating — a higher shelf overlooking the valley where the land opened wide and exposure demanded mindfulness. The climb was narrow and uneven, and more than once Astrid had to brace herself against the stone to keep her balance.

Thorne offered his hand only once — and only when the footing turned perilous.

She took it.

His grip closed around hers, warm and steady, and she felt the familiar flare of awareness stir within her — not spiking, not panicked, but alert.

Contained.

They climbed in silence after that, hands separating when the path allowed. Astrid was acutely aware of the absence — of how easily contact had steadied her, and how carefully they now rationed it.

At the top, the world spread wide before them. Stone fell away into distance, sky stretched pale and open, clouds drifting lazily westward. Wind threaded through Astrid's hair, cool and clean.

"This place remembers choices," Thorne said quietly. "Fewer echoes. Less confusion."

Astrid nodded. "Then it's a good place to practice."

She stepped forward, grounding herself, and reached — not outward, but inward — acknowledging the warmth beneath her ribs, the quiet presence of magic waiting without demand.

The land responded gently.

A patch of lichen brightened against the rock. A fissure smoothed, its edges softening rather than cracking.

Astrid smiled despite herself.

And then she felt it.

A shift.

Not in the magic — but in Thorne.

She opened her eyes.

He stood closer now than he had been all day. Not touching. Not crowding. But undeniable in his nearness, his presence solid and intentional. His gaze wasn't on the horizon anymore.

It was on her.

Astrid's pulse stumbled.

"You're not anchoring," she said quietly.

"No," Thorne replied. "I'm... witnessing."

The word sent a shiver through her that had nothing to do

with the wind.

Astrid stepped closer — not thoughtlessly, but with awareness fully engaged. She felt the magic stir in response, coiling tighter, alert but not straining.

"This feels different," she said. "Last time, it felt like slipping. Like losing footing."

"And now?"

"Like standing at the edge and choosing to stay."

Thorne's breath deepened. "That's the difference between compulsion and desire."

They were close now. Close enough that Astrid could see the subtle tension at the edges of his restraint, the way his shoulders held themselves as if braced against a force no less real for being unseen.

Her heart pounded.

"Thorne," she said softly.

"Yes?"

"I want — " She stopped herself, breath catching. "I want to be honest."

He didn't move. Didn't interrupt.

"I want you," she said simply. Not fiercely. Not desperately. Just truth, laid bare.

The magic surged.

Not violently. Not wildly.

Responsive. Alive.

Thorne closed his eyes for a single heartbeat, as if grounding himself through will alone. When he opened them again, the intensity there made Astrid's knees weaken.

"I want you too," he said.

The words landed like heat spreading through her chest.

For a moment, neither breathed.

Astrid became acutely aware of how little distance remained between them — of how easily she could tip forward, how little effort it would take to close that final inch. The air between them felt dense, charged with something heavier than anticipation.

Her lips parted.

Thorne lifted a hand — slowly, deliberately — and stopped just short of touching her cheek.

The magic coiled tighter, pressure building like a held note.

"This is the moment," he said quietly. "Where we decide."

Astrid's chest tightened painfully. "I know."

"If we cross it now," he continued, "it won't be because we chose it carefully. It will be because it wanted us to."

She nodded, tears pricking unexpectedly at the corners of her eyes. "And I don't want my desire to cost me control."

Thorne's hand lowered — slowly, visibly — until it rested at his side.

"Neither do I."

The decision hurt.

Astrid leaned in anyway — but not to kiss him. Instead, she rested her forehead briefly against his chest, grounding herself through contact that was intimate but restrained. His breath stuttered, then steadied as he allowed it, one hand coming up to rest between her shoulders — open, non-possessive.

The magic responded by quieting.

Peace replaced pressure.

After a long moment, Astrid stepped back.

Their eyes held across the space they had chosen not to close.

"That was… harder than stopping before," she said.

"Yes," Thorne agreed. "Because this time, it was mutual."

"And deliberate."

"Yes."

The word lingered — powerful, anchoring.

They packed up as evening approached, the air cooling again, shadows stretching long across the stone. Astrid felt wrung out, but steadier than she had all day.

As they made camp lower down, she caught herself smiling faintly, chest still aching but no longer hollow.

She looked at Thorne across the firelight. "I don't regret stopping."

"Neither do I," he said without hesitation.

"But I don't regret wanting," she added.

His gaze softened. "You shouldn't."

Night fell gently.

They sat closer than they had before — not touching, but without the rigid boundaries of earlier days. Astrid rested her hands over the earth, feeling its quiet approval beneath her palms.

Desire remained.

So did control.

And Astrid knew — truly knew — that when she finally crossed that line, it would not be because she lost herself.

It would be because she chose, with care, exactly what to claim.

Chapter 14: The Cost of Holding

The morning came clear and cold.

Astrid woke before the sun crested the peaks, breath fogging faintly as she sat up, the world sharply defined in the way it only became after truth had been spoken and not yet answered. The land felt… quiet.

Not dormant. Not withdrawn.

Listening.

She closed her eyes and reached inward — not searching for magic, not testing it — but acknowledging its presence the way one acknowledged their own pulse. It stirred softly, responsive but unstrained.

Something loosened in her chest.

She stood slowly and walked away from camp, boots crunching over frost — stiff grass until she reached a narrow shelf overlooking the valley floor. Pale light spilled over stone and root, turning shadows silver instead of black.

Do not take, she reminded herself.

Ask.

Chapter 14: The Cost of Holding

Astrid knelt and placed both palms flat against the earth.

The magic rose.

Gently.

No spike. No violent press. Just warmth blooming beneath her hands, spreading like sunlight through soil long starved of it. The frost near her fingers retreated, not in haste, but in acceptance.

Astrid gasped.

She didn't pull away.

She breathed.

The earth responded.

Stone smoothed where it had been fractured days earlier, edges rounding as if time itself had been coaxed to move faster — but not recklessly. Moss crept across the rock's surface, green and tentative, life asserting itself without demand.

Astrid laughed softly, disbelief catching in her throat.

"Thorne," she whispered.

His footsteps approached behind her, careful and unhurried.

She didn't turn. "I'm not forcing it."

"I can see that," he said quietly.

The magic hummed — steady. Calm.

Astrid felt tears prickle, chest swelling with something dangerously close to relief. "I'm listening," she said. "And it's answering."

She lifted her hands slowly, and the warmth remained — contained, stable, real.

Silence stretched behind her.

Then Thorne said, reverent and stunned, "You're holding it."

Astrid turned at last.

He stood several paces away, hands open at his sides, posture relaxed in a way she rarely saw — like someone witnessing something sacred rather than guarding against it. His eyes were bright, intent, filled with something close to wonder.

Something in her twisted painfully.

"Come closer," she said, without thinking.

He did.

Not swiftly. Not closed in hunger or urgency. Just present, stepping into her orbit with deliberate care until the space between them felt charged but calm.

The magic didn't surge.

It didn't recoil.

It *settled.*

Astrid swallowed hard. "It's not reacting."

"No," Thorne agreed. "It's… stable."

Her hands trembled — not from strain, but from the enormity of the realization.

"I did it," she whispered. "I didn't break anything. I didn't hurt the land."

She looked up at him, hope blazing bright and fragile. "This changes things."

Thorne's expression softened — but something guarded flickered at its edges.

"Yes," he said carefully. "It does."

The word echoed, colder than she expected.

Astrid's breath caught. "Why do you sound afraid?"

He held her gaze, conflict visibly tightening his jaw. "Because stability means potential."

"And potential is good."

"Potential invites commitment," he said quietly.

The joy in her chest faltered, confusion threading through it. "Thorne — "

"Listen to me," he said gently, stepping back before she could close the distance again. "What you just did — most never manage anything like it. The dragon's trial will no longer be a question of *if*."

Her heart stuttered. "You mean I can return."

"Yes." His voice was steady, but his eyes had gone distant. "And when you do, choices will be demanded. Permanent ones."

The word landed like a weight.

Astrid stared at him. "You think I shouldn't."

"I think," Thorne said slowly, "that success always asks for something in return. And I don't yet know what it will take from you."

"From *us*," she corrected softly.

That stopped him.

Silence stretched, brittle and sharp — edged.

"You don't get to decide that alone," Astrid continued, voice steady despite the ache rising in her chest. "Just like I don't get to pretend this doesn't affect you."

Thorne exhaled, long and tight. "That's exactly what I'm afraid of."

The admission hollowed her.

"You think caring about me will cost you control," she said.

"Yes."

"And you think my magic will demand sacrifice," she pressed. "So you're stepping back before either of us has to choose."

Thorne didn't deny it.

"That's not restraint," Astrid said quietly. "That's retreat."

Pain flashed across his face — brief, but unmistakable.

"I have spent my life preventing damage," he said. "I won't become another thing you have to manage."

Her throat tightened. "I never asked you to."

"No," he said, voice rough. "But I see how the world answers you now. I see what the land expects."

Astrid felt the backlash then — not magic, but grief. Sharp and sudden and deeply unfair.

"Then you don't trust *me*," she said.

He took a step forward, stopped himself, hands curling at his sides. "I trust you more than anyone I've ever known."

"Then trust my choice."

For a long moment, it looked like he might.

The air thrummed, tension thick and humming.

Then Thorne straightened, something closing behind his eyes.

"We should end training early today," he said, formal again. Controlled. "You need rest. This kind of breakthrough — "

Astrid recoiled as if struck.

"So that's it," she whispered. "You pull away the moment things stop being manageable."

His name caught in her throat. "Don't do this."

Thorne looked away. "I need time."

The words felt like stone between her ribs.

Astrid nodded stiffly, fighting the burn behind her eyes. "Fine."

She turned away before he could see her cry — before the magic, responsive and sensitive, could answer the pain with something destructive.

Behind her, the land remained calm.

That hurt most of all.

The rest of the day passed in quiet fracture. They packed camp without speaking, movements efficient but hollow. The connection remained — unbroken — but strained, humming beneath the surface like a fault line denied.

Chapter 14: The Cost of Holding

That night, Astrid sat alone near the fire, hands pressed into the earth.

You listened, the land seemed to say.

Now live with what you heard.

Her magic rested easily within her — for once not the problem, but the mirror.

Across the clearing, Thorne watched the horizon, posture rigid, distance measured with painful care.

They did not speak again before sleep.

But neither pretended the truth away.

Breakthrough had come.

And with it, the first real cost.

Chapter 15: When the Earth Answers Back

The land screamed.

Astrid felt it before the sound reached her ears — a sudden wrenching awareness that tore through her chest like fingers hooked beneath her ribs and pulled outward. She gasped sharply, stumbling one step forward as the ground beneath her feet lurched.

Not violently.

Deliberately.

The stone beneath the clearing vibrated, a low resonant hum rolling outward in widening waves. Loose pebbles skittered across the surface, clattering together as if drawn by something deeper beneath the earth.

Astrid pressed her palm instinctively against the ground.

The connection hit her like a struck chord.

Too loud. Too fast.

Her magic surged in response — not wild, not chaotic — but

urgent, a tight, overwhelming insistence that demanded her attention *now*.

She ripped her hand back. "No — "

The hum deepened.

Across the clearing, Thorne spun toward her, hand flying to the hilt of his sword. "Astrid!"

Before she could answer, the earth heaved.

A deep crack split the stone just beyond the campfire, spreading outward like a spider's web. The ground bulged grotesquely, swelling upward as if something massive were pressing from below. A hot, metallic scent flooded the air — ozone and scorched mineral, sharp enough to sting the lungs.

Astrid staggered back. "This is because of me."

"Eyes up," Thorne barked, already moving.

The ground ruptured.

Stone exploded upward in a violent spray as something massive tore free — a towering shape of jagged rock and molten seams, its body fractured and glowing from within like magma trapped beneath cracked stone. Veins of green-gold light — *her* color — pulsed irregularly through it, too fast, too bright.

Astrid's heart dropped into her stomach.

"By the gods," Thorne muttered. "That's not a wraith."

The construct roared — a sound like a mountain breaking apart — and slammed one massive arm into the ground, sending a shockwave rippling outward.

Astrid was thrown off her feet.

She hit the ground hard, breath ripped from her lungs as she rolled across shattered stone. Pain flared along her injured hand, white and blinding.

Thorne was there instantly.

He hauled her up, one arm braced around her waist, pulling her behind him as another blow cratered the stone meters away.

"Stay behind me," he ordered.

Astrid struggled upright anyway, heart hammering. "It's bound to me," she gasped. "I can feel it — "

The creature turned.

It *felt* her.

The molten veins brightened, flaring in response as the thing pivoted toward her, its great weight crackling the ground beneath it.

Thorne swore violently. "Astrid — move!"

She tried.

Her magic surged instinctively, pressure building fast — *too fast* — as she raised her hands to defend herself.

The land answered.

Not gently.

A wall of stone erupted between her and the creature — but the barrier fractured immediately, collapsing under the construct's brutal weight. The effort tore a cry from Astrid's throat as pain speared up her arms.

"No," she whispered, panic rising. "I'm losing it — "

Thorne turned back toward her, eyes burning. "You're not."

He took her by the shoulders, hard enough to hurt. "Astrid — look at me."

She locked eyes with him.

The chaos dimmed.

"Breathe," he commanded. "Don't push. Don't *fix*. Listen."

Her breath shuddered — but she obeyed.

The magic quivered, strained but responsive.

The creature surged forward with another roar, raising both

arms to strike.

Thorne moved without hesitation.

He shoved Astrid backward — then turned and met the thing head-on.

His sword rang uselessly against the creature's stony hide, sparks cascading as the impact jarred through him. The construct backhanded him across the clearing with crushing force.

"THORNE!"

Astrid screamed his name as he skidded across shattered ground, armor scraping stone, coming to a brutal stop meters away.

Pain flooded her system.

The magic exploded in response.

Green-gold light surged outward from her in a violent wave, the ground buckling and cracking beneath her feet. Roots tore free from the stone, lashing upward, wrapping around the creature's legs in jagged coils.

The construct bellowed — but the power fueling Astrid's spell spiked dangerously fast.

Too fast.

Her vision dimmed at the edges.

This is how it happens, she realized in a cold flash of understanding. *This is how I lose control again.*

"No," she whispered fiercely. "Not like this."

She dropped to one knee, slamming her uninjured palm against the earth.

You listened, the land had said.

Now it was *asking* something back.

Astrid forced herself to speak — not a command, not a prayer — but a promise.

"I acknowledge what I've changed," she gasped. "Help me correct it."

The magic responded.

Not by growing stronger.

By *slowing*.

The surging light compressed, drawing inward instead of outward. Pressure built, heavy and painful, but contained.

Astrid cried out as the strain tore through her — but she held.

The roots binding the creature thickened, stone hardening around them as the land obeyed her control rather than her panic. The construct thrashed violently, molten seams flashing brighter as it fought to break free.

Astrid staggered upright, drenched in sweat, arms shaking violently.

She took one step toward Thorne.

Then another.

The creature roared again, ripping one leg free from the stone.

Manual control won't hold much longer, she realized.

She needed an anchor.

"Thorne!" she shouted.

He stirred — strained but conscious — dragging himself to one knee.

His eyes found hers.

"Together," she said hoarsely.

He understood instantly.

Thorne planted his sword into the soil and braced himself, feet wide, posture solid. "Come here."

Astrid didn't hesitate.

She ran.

The moment she came within reach, he seized her wrist — firm, grounding — and pulled her against his side, one arm locking around her shoulders as he became a living wall.

The magic reacted immediately — pressure spiking dangerously.

Astrid nearly screamed —

— but this time, she didn't shove it away.

She acknowledged it *with him*.

"Breathe with me," Thorne said, voice rough but steady against her ear.

She matched his inhale.

Out.

In.

The magic stabilized.

The roots binding the creature strengthened, stone sealing more deliberately around its thrashing form. The land quieted — not obedient, but cooperative.

The construct let out one final, furious roar as the earth dragged it downward, stone closing deliberately around it until only fractured ground remained.

Silence slammed into the clearing.

Astrid collapsed against Thorne, every muscle shaking violently as the magic drained away.

He caught her fully this time, arms wrapping around her without restraint, without hesitation.

She clutched his armor, breath coming in ragged gasps. "I couldn't stop it alone."

"I know," he said hoarsely.

They stayed like that for several long moments, the land settling beneath them, fine dust drifting down from cracked stone.

Astrid pulled back first.

Her vision was swimming, exhaustion pulsing through her veins — but clarity burned sharp beneath it.

"That thing," she said. "It wasn't random."

"No," Thorne agreed grimly. "It answered you."

"I *made* it possible," she said, pain tightening her chest. "My balance shifted the land — and this rose to compensate."

Thorne studied the fractured ground where the creature had vanished. "Then your power isn't just reactive anymore," he said. "It's formative."

The weight of the word crushed down on her.

"I don't get to pretend this is just my problem," Astrid whispered. "Every step I take changes the world."

His gaze softened, fierce and conflicted. "That's the burden of real power."

She swallowed hard. "And now you see why I can't do this alone."

"Yes."

The word hung between them.

"I tried to step back," Thorne continued quietly. "Because I was afraid of binding your path to mine."

Astrid held his gaze. "You were already bound the moment you chose to stand with me."

Something cracked in his expression.

"This — " she gestured weakly toward the scarred earth, the shattered clearing, the place where a living mountain had risen " — this is what happens when we pretend proximity is optional."

Thorne closed his eyes briefly, then opened them with resolve etched into every line of him.

"I won't retreat again," he said. "Not without your consent."

Her breath hitched.

"And I won't deny what I need to stay balanced," Astrid replied. "Even when it frightens me."

They stood together in the wreckage, the land quiet beneath them once more — but changed.

The storm had passed.

But the world had noticed.

Far beneath their feet, something deep and ancient shifted — measuring, remembering.

The Dragon would feel this.

Astrid knew it with terrible certainty.

Breakthrough had come.

So had consequence.

And from this moment forward, nothing would rise to meet her without demanding she meet it *in return*.

They did not go far before Thorne called a halt.

Not because the land demanded it, but because Astrid's body finally did. The tension that had carried her through containment ebbed away all at once, leaving behind trembling limbs and the hollow ache that followed too much power held too tightly.

They found a shallow hollow in the stone and built a fire that was more ember than flame.

Astrid sat with her back against the rock, cloak drawn close, hands resting in her lap because she didn't trust them to do anything else.

Thorne moved around her with quiet efficiency — checking the ground, testing the rock, setting his sword within reach. He didn't speak until the fire steadied.

Then he crouched in front of her.

"Look at me," he said quietly.

Not command.

Request.

Astrid lifted her gaze.

His eyes were steady, but something tight lived beneath the calm — as if restraint had been pulled closer around him rather than released.

"You didn't lose control," Thorne said.

Astrid swallowed. "I almost did."

"But you didn't."

She exhaled shakily. "Because you were there."

Thorne didn't deny it. He didn't claim it.

He shifted closer, slow enough to give her time to object. His hand came up — not to her face, not to anywhere that would alter the meaning of the moment.

It settled on her forearm.

Warm. Solid. Still.

Astrid froze — not with fear, but with sudden, piercing awareness.

The magic inside her stirred instantly, attentive but calm, as if waiting to see what *she* would choose.

Thorne's thumb moved once, barely a confirmation.

Her breath caught.

"Thorne," she whispered.

"Yes."

"I don't know what to do with this," she admitted.

Not the magic.

Him.

His gaze held hers. "You don't need to do anything with it tonight."

Astrid let out a small, incredulous sound. "That sounds like permission."

"It is," Thorne said.

The fire cracked softly.

Astrid realized she was leaning toward him, just barely — enough that stepping closer would require effort, not impulse.

She stopped herself.

Not denial.

Choice.

Thorne didn't close the distance.

He didn't retreat from it either.

He let the space between them exist exactly as she set it.

The restraint made her chest ache.

"If we keep doing this," Astrid said quietly, "if I keep needing you to stabilize — "

"You're not needing me," Thorne interrupted gently. "You're choosing partnership."

The words landed clean and undeniable.

Astrid inhaled sharply. "And what are you doing?"

Thorne's gaze dropped to her mouth for a heartbeat — unmistakable — before returning to her eyes.

"The same," he said.

Silence pressed between them, dense and charged.

Astrid could feel the moment balancing on a knife's edge. One step. One lean. One decision.

She leaned forward — just enough to thin the air between them.

Thorne's breath hitched.

For a suspended heartbeat, crossing that last inch would have been effortless.

Astrid stopped.

Not because she was afraid.

Because she wanted the first time to be deliberate. Hers.

"Not tonight," she whispered.

Thorne closed his eyes briefly, as if bracing against that truth rather than resisting it.

"Not tonight," he agreed.

He withdrew his hand slowly, carefully, like he was setting down something fragile instead of retreating.

The absence was immediate and sharp.

Her magic did not react.

That mattered.

Thorne rose and resumed watch — but he did not put distance in the space behind her. He stayed close enough that his warmth still touched the edge of her awareness.

Astrid stared into the low fire until her breathing steadied.

Nothing had happened.

And yet everything had.

For the first time, she understood that restraint could be intimate.

That refusal could be desire made deliberate.

And that when they finally crossed that line, it would not be because necessity forced them there —

but because they chose it with eyes open.

Chapter 16: What Must Be Carried Forward

The land did not heal itself overnight.

Astrid knew that the moment she woke.

The quiet that greeted dawn was not the calm patience she had learned to recognize, but something thinner — strained, as though the earth were holding its breath after shouting too loudly and finding itself suddenly heard.

She rose slowly from where she'd slept near the edge of the broken clearing, muscles still sore, magic heavy beneath her skin but mercifully still. The ground bore the scars of the day before: long fissures stitched clumsily together by stone that had not yet decided whether it wished to remain whole.

She swallowed hard.

I did this.

Not in the reckless way she once might have feared — but in a deeper, more unsettling sense. Her breakthrough had not healed the land. It had *changed* it. Set something in motion that would not simply settle back into what it had been before.

Across the clearing, Thorne was already awake, methodically inspecting his armor where it had cracked beneath the construct's blow. He hadn't spoken much since the battle — neither apology nor reassurance, just presence and pragmatic motion, as if words were too fragile for a truth this heavy.

Astrid crossed the distance between them, boots crunching softly over fractured stone.

"Does it look worse in the daylight?" she asked quietly.

Thorne glanced up, golden eyes thoughtful rather than alarmed. "It looks honest."

She winced. "That bad?"

"No," he said. "That clear."

He set a dented strap aside and stood, towering as ever but no longer looming. His gaze swept the ruined clearing, the sealed fissure where the construct had been swallowed whole.

"This wasn't corruption," he continued. "Not entirely. It was imbalance taking form."

Astrid folded her arms around herself. "Because of me."

"Because of what you *changed*," he corrected gently. "And because the world answers change."

She pressed her palm to the stone at her side, grounding herself through habit now rather than desperation. The earth responded faintly — not pushing, not pulling — simply acknowledging.

"It answered faster than I was ready for," she said. "I don't think I would have survived that alone."

"You wouldn't have needed to," Thorne said flatly.

She met his gaze. "Then say it."

He didn't pretend not to understand.

"We can no longer treat your training as something that

happens in isolation," he said. "Your presence is now a variable the land reacts to. That means every step we take, every place we rest, every choice you make — it all carries weight beyond us."

"And beyond recovery," Astrid added quietly.

"Yes."

The word settled between them, heavy as stone.

Astrid drew a long breath. "Then let's stop pretending the Dragon's Tearstone is optional."

Thorne stilled.

This time, he didn't retreat.

"I was hoping you wouldn't say that so soon," he admitted.

"I was hoping I wouldn't feel so certain," she replied.

They stood in silence for a moment, the wind threading softly through broken grass, the world waiting in that peculiar way it had adopted since Astrid's magic had learned to speak more clearly.

"When I knelt yesterday," Astrid continued, "I didn't ask the earth to protect me. I acknowledged the change I'd made and asked how to correct it." Her throat tightened. "It answered by showing me what happens if I hesitate."

Thorne nodded grimly. "Power that teaches responsibility does so violently when ignored."

"That creature," Astrid said, "wasn't punishment. It was consequence — a counterweight."

"And there will be more," Thorne said.

"Yes."

The certainty between them was absolute.

Astrid lowered herself onto a half — intact stone slab, exhaustion finally seeping through resolve. "Then I need to return to the dragon not because I want a cure — but because the land won't stabilize until I understand the full cost of what I've become."

Thorne crouched in front of her again, familiar now not as guardian, but as anchor.

"And you need protection while you do it," he said.

She met his gaze without flinching. "No. I need *partnership*."

The word hung between them, no longer hypothetical.

Thorne exhaled slowly. "This path will ask something of both of us."

"I know." Her voice was steady despite the ache behind it. "I won't pretend otherwise. But I won't walk it with you holding yourself apart as if distance keeps either of us safe."

He considered that — really considered it.

"You nearly died yesterday," he said quietly.

"So did you."

"That doesn't mean I accept the risk."

"No," Astrid said gently. "But it means you can't prevent it by stepping away."

Something settled in his expression then — not surrender, but decision.

"Very well," he said. "Then we plan."

Relief and fear tangled painfully in her chest.

They spent the rest of the morning doing just that.

Mapping the terrain ahead. Naming fault lines where Astrid's magic might provoke response. Establishing clear signals — words, touches, distance markers — to manage proximity without denial or indulgence. It was methodical, careful work, threaded through with an unspoken understanding that emotion was not the enemy — *ignorance* was.

At one point, Astrid shook visibly, fatigue finally asserting itself.

Thorne noticed immediately. He stood beside her, close but not touching. "You're burning through reserves faster now."

"Yes," she admitted. "Holding stability takes... more than it used to."

"That will change," he said. "Skill reduces cost."

"And until then?"

"We manage."

She smiled faintly. "You say that like it's simple."

"It's not," he replied. "But it's familiar."

By midday, the land felt quieter — not healed, but no longer agitated. They broke camp carefully, leaving markers along the path to avoid grounding faults and unstable seams.

As they moved, Astrid felt the subtle pull again — the sense of being watched, weighed, remembered.

The Dragon feels this, she thought.

And beyond that —

"What happens if I choose not to take the Tear?" she asked suddenly.

Thorne slowed, turning to face her fully.

"That's a real question," he said.

"I mean it," she pressed. "If the Dragon offers it as a cure, but taking it solidifies my magic in ways I'm not prepared to live with... what then?"

Thorne studied her with something close to pride. "Then you will have more power than most gods ever grant mortals."

She snorted weakly. "That's not comforting."

"It should be," he said. "Because it means choice remains yours."

Her gaze softened.

They stopped at the ridge as evening approached — a vantage point overlooking miles of terrain they had already crossed, the land behind them marked subtly by her passage.

Astrid rested her hands over her abdomen, feeling the quiet, contained weight of her power.

"It didn't rage today," she said.

"No."

"It didn't answer without invitation."

"No."

She looked at Thorne. "That means I can live with this."

Thorne's voice was low. "It also means the world will hold you to what you've claimed."

She nodded. "That's fair."

The sun dipped low, bathing everything in amber light. For a moment, Astrid allowed herself to feel the dangerous thing she'd been denying all day — the comfort of his nearness, the steadiness that did not disrupt her magic but seemed to steady it.

She didn't act on it.

Neither did he.

But neither stepped away.

As night fell, Astrid understood something plainly for the first time since leaving the temple:

Curses did not demand isolation.

Power did not demand solitude.

The road ahead would be unforgiving — but it would not be walked alone.

And when the Dragon finally answered her, Astrid would not come seeking absolution.

She would come ready to decide what she was willing to carry.

Chapter 17: The One Who Heard the Change

Astrid felt the watcher before she saw them.

It wasn't the familiar weight of the earth's attention — a patient, listening presence she had begun to recognize — but something sharper, directional. Focused. The sensation pricked along the back of her neck like a held breath not her own.

She slowed instinctively.

Thorne noticed at once.

"What is it?" he murmured, hand drifting closer to his sword without touching it.

"We're not alone," Astrid whispered. "And whoever it is… they're not hiding from the land. They're *listening* to it."

Thorne's gaze swept the ridgeline ahead — stone rising in uneven tiers, scattered brush clinging stubbornly to incline and fracture. Nothing moved. The air lay still.

"Human?" he asked quietly.

"Not entirely," Astrid said. "Or not only."

The pressure sharpened.

A step crunched deliberately against stone.

Astrid turned just as the figure emerged from behind a narrow spur of rock — unhurried, unarmed, and utterly unconcerned with concealment.

They were tall and spare, wrapped in layered travel-worn robes that smelled faintly of old ash and rain. Pale markings traced their exposed hands and throat — sigils, Astrid realized dimly, not carved or inked, but *grown*, like veins of light pressed just beneath skin.

The stranger stopped several paces away and inclined their head.

"You felt it too quickly," the figure said. "That confirms it."

Thorne put himself half a step in front of Astrid, posture unmistakably defensive. "Confirm what?"

The stranger's gaze slid past him without dismissal but without deference, settling on Astrid with unmistakable intent.

"That the shift was not accidental," they said. "And that it came from you."

Astrid's heart began to pound.

"You felt the construct rise," Astrid said, more question than accusation.

"I felt the *answer*," the figure corrected. "The land does not always scream — but when it moves that deliberately, those who listen cannot pretend otherwise."

Thorne's voice hardened. "You'll state your name and your purpose."

A faint smile touched the stranger's mouth — not mocking, but edged with something weary.

"I am Sylvae," they said. "A Warden of the Sleeping Places.

And my purpose, Guardian, has already occurred."

Astrid's breath caught. "Wardens are a myth."

"They prefer it that way," Sylvae replied mildly.

Thorne didn't move. "You approached armed only with certainty," he said. "That makes you dangerous."

"Yes," Sylvae agreed. "But not today."

They turned their attention fully to Astrid then, eyes startlingly clear — too clear, as if layers of the visible world had been peeled away.

"You reshaped a fault," Sylvae said. "Contained a formative echo. Bound and quieted an answering construct without collapsing the lattice beneath it."

Astrid stiffened. "That information isn't yours."

"It is when it threatens to repeat," Sylvae said. "When the land changes its language, we pay attention."

The air seemed to tighten around them — not hostile, but *alert.*

Thorne shifted slightly closer to Astrid. She felt it immediately — the anchoring presence, the familiar steadiness. Her magic stirred, then settled.

Sylvae noticed.

Their brows lifted minutely. "Interesting."

"What?" Astrid demanded.

"Proximity," Sylvae said. "Not dominance. Not suppression. Stabilization." Their gaze flicked briefly to Thorne, then back to Astrid. "That is… unusual."

Thorne bristled. "You're observing us like curiosities."

"I observe patterns," Sylvae replied. "Curiosity comes later."

Astrid drew a slow breath. "If you're a Warden, then you know why I'm here."

"Yes," Sylvae said. "You seek the Dragon's Tearstone."

Thorne's hand closed around empty air where his sword hung. "You will not speak of that lightly."

"I don't," Sylvae replied. "Which is why I'm telling you now: the Dragon will not be the only one responding to what you've changed."

Astrid's pulse spiked. "Others felt it."

"Yes." Sylvae's gaze hardened. "Some who will ask permission. Some who will not."

Silence stretched tight and brittle.

Thorne spoke first. "Then you're here to stop her."

"No," Sylvae said flatly. "If I were, this conversation would already be over."

Astrid's stomach clenched. "Then why are you here?"

Sylvae considered her for a long moment. "Because containment without witness becomes corruption. And because what you're becoming — " they paused, choosing words carefully, " — requires more than solitary judgment."

"I don't need a handler," Astrid snapped.

"Nor do we offer one," Sylvae said. "We offer context."

They gestured toward the fractured valley behind them — the subtle signs Astrid now noticed more easily than she dared admit. "Your power has moved from responsive to declarative. The land will remember you now."

Astrid swallowed. "That doesn't make me a threat."

"No," Sylvae agreed softly. "But it makes you *relevant*."

That word landed like a stone dropped into deep water.

Thorne shook his head. "If you're not here to impede us, then state your intent plainly."

Sylvae turned at last to meet his gaze directly. "To warn you. And to measure."

Astrid stiffened. "Measure me."

"Yes."

Her magic stirred, offended — not lashing, but taut.

"I won't submit to assessment," she said.

Sylvae inclined their head again. "Good. Anyone who would is not suited to what lies ahead."

The tension fractured into something sharper.

"If others felt it," Astrid said carefully, "then waiting only worsens the imbalance."

Sylvae studied her approvingly. "You understand consequence."

"I have to."

"Then hear this," Sylvae said, voice quieting the space around them. "Returning to the Dragon without acknowledging the watching forces will provoke intervention. Some benevolent. Some… less so."

Thorne's jaw tightened. "And you expect us to simply accept the scrutiny."

"No," Sylvae said. "I expect you to choose how visible you wish to be."

Astrid laughed suddenly, brittle and humorless. "That choice passed the moment the earth answered me."

"Yes," Sylvae said gently. "Which is why you are no longer alone in this, whether you wish it or not."

The truth of it hit hard.

"So what now?" Astrid asked.

Sylvae's gaze flicked between them — assessing not just Astrid, but the space she shared with Thorne.

"Now," Sylvae said, "you continue. Toward the Dragon. Toward decision." They took one step back. "And we watch."

Thorne's voice dropped low. "From where?"

"From wherever the land listens," Sylvae replied. "And when

it speaks too loudly again — "

"You'll intervene," Thorne finished.

"We'll appear," Sylvae corrected. "Intervention remains your choice."

With that, the Warden turned — already fading into the terrain, presence dissolving into stone and wind like a thought released.

Astrid stood motionless long after they were gone.

Her hands trembled — not with magic, but with implication.

Thorne broke the silence first. "You held your ground."

"I didn't feel like I had another option," Astrid said faintly.

He stepped closer. "Do you regret it?"

She shook her head. "I regret that the world is larger than I thought. And less patient."

Thorne exhaled slowly. "You're not facing it blindly anymore."

"No," she said. "But now we're being seen."

The weight of that truth pressed heavily between them.

"I won't let them decide for you," Thorne said firmly.

Astrid looked up at him — really looked at him — and felt, with sharp clarity, how different this felt from his earlier retreat.

"I don't want them to," she said. "But I also won't pretend I can ignore them."

They stood together a moment longer, the land quiet but attentive beneath their feet.

Somewhere far beyond the horizon, ancient eyes were opening.

And Astrid understood with sober certainty:

The next steps would define more than her fate.

They would define how the world remembered her.

Chapter 18: Where Silence Listens

The first thing Astrid noticed was the quiet.

Not the absence of sound — that she had learned could be deceptive — but the kind of quiet that *waited*. The land lay still beneath a sky washed pale with the remains of storm, stone and root holding themselves in a careful balance as if any careless gesture might set something moving again.

She sat at the edge of camp, knees drawn up beneath her cloak, hands pressed lightly to the earth more out of habit than need. Her magic remained calm — coiled, attentive, decidedly *awake* — but it did not press. It simply watched the world through her senses.

That alone unsettled her.

Behind her, Thorne sharpened one of his blades with slow, methodical strokes. The sound should have been comforting by now, a rhythm she associated with preparedness and safety. Instead, it prickled along her awareness, every rasp of stone against metal cutting clean through the stillness.

Not because of him.

Because of who else might hear it.

Astrid drew a slow breath.

"They're still here," she said quietly.

The blade paused mid — stroke.

"I know," Thorne replied.

He didn't ask *who*. After Sylvae's appearance, the land no longer felt like something that belonged solely to them. Awareness lingered at the edges now — faint, not hostile, but undeniably present. The sense that something vast had shifted its attention and was waiting to see what would follow.

Astrid hated it.

Not fear exactly — she could already handle fear — but the intrusion of it. The way her thoughts no longer felt wholly her own, every flicker of emotion answering a world that now listened too closely.

Thorne set the blade aside and moved closer, stopping short of touching her, posture open rather than guarded.

"You don't have to hold everything inside yourself," he said. "Not with this."

Astrid lifted her gaze to his. "I don't know what's safe anymore."

He considered that. "Safe from harm, or safe from being seen?"

She swallowed. "Is there a difference?"

Thorne didn't answer immediately. Instead, he sat beside her — close enough that their shoulders nearly brushed, far enough that the space between them still felt like a conversation rather than an assumption.

"That depends," he said finally, "on whether being seen changes what you choose."

Astrid looked back to the land. "I don't want my restraint

to turn into theater. I don't want to live like every honest moment has to be guarded because someone *might* interpret it."

Thorne's jaw tightened. "Nor should you."

She glanced at him sharply. "Then why do I feel like the moment I reach for you, it stops being mine?"

The silence pressed close.

Thorne turned to face her fully. "Because you're aware now that meaning travels further than intent."

"That doesn't make it fair."

"No." His voice softened. "But it does make it real."

Astrid closed her eyes, frustration building — not with him, not even with the watchers, but with herself. With the part of her that wanted, fiercely and unapologetically, to claim space that did not yet belong safely to her.

"I need one thing to be clear," she said, opening her eyes again. "Whatever happens between us — whatever doesn't — I won't let it be dictated by fear of being observed."

Thorne studied her carefully. "And if what you choose draws attention?"

She met his gaze. "Then attention will have to learn restraint too."

A beat passed.

Then, slowly, deliberately, Thorne shifted closer and sat fully beside her. This time, there was no space left unspoken. His presence at her side was unmistakable, solid, chosen.

Astrid felt the magic stir at once — not spiking, not threatening — but alert, as if marking a boundary crossed with intention rather than impulse.

The land responded with a low, subtle hum.

Astrid tensed instinctively.

Thorne noticed immediately. He didn't move away — but he tilted his head slightly, listening with her.

The hum steadied.

"That wasn't interference," he murmured. "That was… acknowledgment."

Astrid frowned. "You felt it."

"Yes."

She let out a breath. "Then it's not just me being watched."

"No," Thorne agreed. "It's *us* being understood."

The implication curled tight in her chest.

"So even silence speaks now," she said quietly.

"Yes."

She laughed once, quietly and without humor. "That seems unfair."

Thorne smiled faintly. "The land has never been particularly concerned with fairness."

They sat there for a long moment, neither speaking, the air between them charged not with urgency but with awareness sharpened to a fine edge.

Astrid became keenly conscious of the way Thorne's arm rested close to hers — not touching, but warm enough that she could feel the heat through layers of cloth. Every instinct urged her to lean in, but for once, she didn't suppress it.

She acknowledged it.

"I don't regret wanting this," she said softly. "Not you. Not closeness. But I hate that it feels like a signal flare."

Thorne's voice was low, steady. "You're not wrong to want privacy."

"Wanting it doesn't make it real."

"No," he said. "But choosing *how* to be seen does."

She turned toward him, frustration giving way to something

sharper. "And what if what I choose is... quiet intimacy. Things said softly. Touch without spectacle."

"Then you make that choice consciously," Thorne said. "And you don't shrink it just because someone might notice."

Astrid searched his face. "And if those watching decide to judge?"

"Let them," Thorne said flatly. "Judgment without influence is just noise."

The certainty in his voice grounded her more than any spell could have.

She shifted slightly and rested her head back against the stone, close enough now that her sleeve brushed his armor when the wind moved just so. The magic stirred again, curious rather than demanding.

Astrid focused — not on control, but on permission.

The hum of the land softened.

She swallowed. "Then let this be something we choose — not something we hide."

Thorne exhaled slowly. "Agreed."

They spoke quietly after that — not in confessions or declarations, but in shared understanding. About the road ahead. About the Dragon. About the knowledge that whatever waited for Astrid there would no longer belong to her alone.

At one point, she turned toward him without thinking, forehead nearly brushing his shoulder before she caught herself.

The magic tightened.

Astrid froze.

Then loosened.

She let herself rest there — not leaning fully, not retreating — existing in the space between.

Thorne didn't move away.

Nor did he touch her.

The restraint was deliberate. Mutual. Achingly precise.

Astrid felt the presence at the edge of awareness again then — not closer, not louder, but attentive. As if someone, somewhere, had noticed the difference between suppression and choice.

She didn't flinch.

Instead, she spoke softly, deliberately, into the open air.

"This isn't secrecy," she said. "It's care."

The land answered with stillness.

Thorne angled his head toward her, voice barely above breath. "Do you feel that?"

"Yes," she whispered. "They're listening."

"And not interrupting."

"That's new."

"Yes," he said. "It is."

For the first time since Sylvae appeared, Astrid felt something loosen in her chest.

They weren't hiding.

They weren't performing.

They were simply *being*, with intention sharp enough to be seen without being taken.

When darkness finally crept in, they made camp closer than they had before — still separate, still restrained, but without fear of acknowledgment. The fire burned low and steady, the earth beneath them quiet and accepting.

As Astrid lay down to rest, staring up at a sky heavy with stars, she realized something that surprised her.

Being watched did not make intimacy impossible.

It made **choice** unavoidable.

And somewhere beyond sight, those who listened learned something important that night:

Astrid did not deny herself.

She decided.

Chapter 19: The Mistake They Made

Astrid felt the judgment before she understood it.

It settled over the land like a breath drawn too sharply — subtle, almost polite, but unmistakably evaluative. Not curiosity. Not caution.

Assessment.

She slowed mid — step, fingers curling reflexively into her cloak. Her magic responded with irritation — not surging, not defensive, but taut, as if bracing against a frame that did not fit.

"They've decided something," she said quietly.

Thorne's stride faltered beside her. "About you?"

Astrid shook her head once. "About *us*."

The word felt weighted now — larger than intimacy, larger than confession. It carried implication. Visibility.

Thorne angled slightly closer without touching, posture marking boundary rather than defense. "Tell me what you feel."

"Expectation," Astrid replied after a moment. "Like a hand

reaching toward a mechanism they think they understand."

The air cooled abruptly.

Stone to their left darkened, faint lines shimmering across its surface like frost that hadn't yet decided whether to form. Astrid's pulse picked up — not from fear, but anger.

"No," she murmured. "That isn't yours."

A presence stepped out of the terrain as if from behind a veil that had never fully lifted.

It wasn't Sylvae this time.

This figure wore the earth differently — less like a traveler, more like a function given form. Their robes were pale gray, barely distinct from the mist curling around their feet. No sigils marked their skin. Instead, the impression of law clung to them, heavy and automatic.

They regarded Astrid with calm certainty.

"So," the watcher said. "You are the axis."

Astrid felt it then — the misinterpretation snapping into place.

"No," Astrid said evenly. "I'm not."

The watcher's gaze flicked briefly to Thorne, then back. "You are constrained," they said. "Restrained by proximity and dependency. That makes you volatile."

Thorne stiffened — but Astrid stepped forward before he could speak.

"That conclusion is incorrect."

The figure tilted their head slightly. "You deny evidence?"

Astrid lifted her chin. "I deny your interpretation."

"You hold power that reconfigures the lattice," the watcher said. "Your restraint does not arise from mastery. It arises from suppression."

Astrid laughed once, sharp and joyless. "That's a convenient assumption."

"What you describe as choice," the watcher continued, "bears all the markers of imposed limitation. You pause when drawn toward intimacy. You divert when alignment intensifies. You fragment integration pathways rather than commit."

Astrid's magic *bristled*.

"That is *restraint*," the watcher concluded. "And restraint under coercion always fails."

Thorne's voice dropped low. "You'll watch your accusations."

For the first time, the watcher looked at Thorne fully.

"And you," they said, "are the coercive vector."

The words struck hard — and wrong.

Astrid moved then, stepping fully between them without touching either.

"Enough," she said.

The land went still.

The watcher blinked — just once. "You intercede."

"I assert," Astrid corrected. "There is a difference."

She felt the land respond — not sharply, not violently, but in deep agreement. The pressure around them eased once, like a held breath released.

"You see proximity and assume dominance," Astrid continued. "You see restraint and assume fear. You mistake consent for submission."

The watcher's brows furrowed minutely. "Language barriers are common in emergent phenomena."

Astrid's hands trembled — not with magic, but with fury carefully held.

"No," she said. "What's common is observers mistaking silence for absence of will."

She inhaled slowly, grounding herself the way she now knew

how.

"My magic stabilizes when I choose honesty over impulse," Astrid said. "When I choose closeness with care, not avoidance from fear."

The watcher turned slightly, regarding her anew. "And yet you refrain."

"Yes," Astrid said. "Because I choose *when*, not because someone tells me *whether*."

She met Thorne's gaze briefly — just long enough for the truth to pass between them — then returned her attention to the watcher.

"You believe restraint equals captivity," Astrid said. "That tells me far more about your framework than mine."

The watcher was silent for several beats.

Interesting, Astrid thought — not convinced, but destabilized.

"And you," the watcher said at last, addressing Thorne again, "if not limiting her, are you willing to accept the consequences of unmediated convergence?"

Thorne didn't hesitate.

"I am willing to support what she chooses," he said. "Including restraint."

The watcher's eyes sharpened. "Even if it costs her opportunity."

"Even if it costs *me* proximity," Thorne replied calmly.

Astrid's chest tightened painfully at the words — not rejection, but respect made explicit.

"That answer contradicts expectation," the watcher said.

"Then update it," Astrid snapped.

Silence cracked outward.

The mist thickened briefly around the watcher's form, as

though the land itself were shifting position to listen more closely.

"You assert autonomy," the watcher said slowly. "Yet the risk profile remains unacceptable."

Astrid's patience snapped.

She stepped closer — not threatening, but unmistakably present.

"You think I'm being restrained because I'm afraid of my power," Astrid said. "You think I'm holding back because intimacy destabilizes me."

She shook her head. "You're wrong. I hold back because I *respect* what stability costs."

The watcher regarded her intently.

"I am not a danger because I pause," Astrid continued. "I'm dangerous if I don't."

Thorne felt the land answer then — a low, resonant hum that rolled outward across the stone like approval rendered audible. Not allegiance.

Recognition.

The watcher faltered — just a flicker.

"That response contradicts historical models," they said.

"Then your models are outdated," Astrid replied coolly.

A long silence followed.

Finally, the watcher stepped back — not retreating, but recalibrating.

"You are not suppressed," they said slowly. "You are... deliberate."

Astrid didn't soften. "Now you're listening."

The watcher inclined their head, not in submission, but acknowledgment.

"We will revise assessment parameters," they said. "Intervention is deferred."

With that, the presence withdrew — not vanishing, but receding into the layers of land and air that now seemed unable to ignore Astrid entirely.

The clearing remained still long after they were gone.

Astrid exhaled shakily.

"That," she said, "was infuriating."

Thorne let out a breath he hadn't realized he was holding. "You were extraordinary."

She turned toward him, eyes bright with lingering anger. "They thought you were controlling me."

"I know."

"They assumed restraint meant fear."

"I know."

She stepped closer — not touching, but close enough that the choice was unmistakable.

"I need you to hear this clearly," Astrid said. "I choose restraint. I choose timing. I choose *you* being part of the process — not the reason it exists."

Thorne's expression softened, fierce with something deep and steady. "I never doubted that."

"Then don't let anyone else doubt it either."

"Never again," he said firmly.

They stood together in the aftermath, the land quieter now — not silent, but recalibrated.

Astrid felt something settle — not relief, but authority.

The watchers had misread her.

They wouldn't again.

Because now she was no longer merely responding to what observed her.

She was **defining the terms under which she would be**

seen.

And that, she knew with certainty, would change everything that came next.

Chapter 20: The Direction of Consequence

The land changed its tone.

Astrid sensed it not as pressure, but as alignment — a subtle narrowing of possibility that made certain paths feel heavier than others. The air carried purpose now, as if choices had been cataloged and weighed, and the remaining options laid bare with quiet insistence.

She paused at the edge of a shallow rise, hand resting lightly against a stone worn smooth by countless seasons.

"This is new," she said.

Thorne stopped beside her. "What kind of new?"

"Decisive," Astrid replied. "The land isn't asking questions anymore."

She closed her eyes, letting her awareness expand just enough to touch the terrain ahead. The sensation that met her was unmistakable: a pull — not coercive, not violent — but firm, directional.

Like a road revealed after the fog lifts.

"It wants me moving," she said softly. "East. Higher. Toward the mountains."

Thorne didn't smile, but something settled in his posture. "Toward the Dragon."

"Yes."

They stood in silence for a long moment, the weight of inevitability pressing no harder than it had to.

"They're reacting to what you said yesterday," Thorne said at last.

Astrid nodded. "So am I."

She straightened, resolve threading through fatigue. The magic within her stirred — not surging, not testing boundaries — but attentive, poised like a held breath ready to be released with care.

"Before, I thought returning to the Dragon was something I chose when I was ready," she said. "Now I think readiness is what happens when delay becomes irresponsible."

Thorne studied the mountain line in the distance, eyes narrowed against the glare. "You're certain."

"Yes."

He glanced at her then — not searching for doubt, but acknowledging commitment. "Then we adjust our pace."

They traveled hard that day.

The terrain steepened quickly, ridgelines folding into one another as if the land itself were tightening the path. Astrid felt watched again — not with judgment this time, but awareness sharpened by interest.

Not all watchers disapproved, she realized.

Some were *waiting*.

Midway through the afternoon, Astrid faltered briefly — not

from exhaustion, but reaction. The stone beneath her boots pulsed once, sharp and brief.

She caught herself instantly.

Thorne moved closer, not touching, voice low. "What did it do?"

"Marked," Astrid said. "Not me. The direction."

She knelt and placed her palm to the ground, focusing carefully.

A faint line of warmth extended ahead — subtle, nearly invisible, but deliberate. A path traced not in force, but resonance.

Thorne frowned. "That wasn't there before."

"No," Astrid replied. "It's not guidance. It's… confirmation."

She rose, brushing dust from her hands.

"They're no longer evaluating whether I should continue," she said grimly. "They're preparing for what happens when I arrive."

Thorne exhaled slowly. "Then whatever price the Dragon asks won't be theoretical either."

Astrid's jaw tightened. "No."

They didn't speak much after that, their silence shaped not by tension, but by shared focus. The road narrowed, air thinning as elevation crept upward. The world felt taller here — older, less accommodating.

As dusk fell, they made camp beneath a jutting shelf of rock streaked with mineral lines that shimmered faintly under Astrid's gaze.

"This place is stable," she said quietly. "But it's listening."

Thorne nodded. "Most places are now."

They ate in measured quiet, each lost to thought. Astrid felt the weight of her choice settle — not crushing, but profound.

This was the point of no return, she understood — not because she couldn't turn back, but because doing so would now be its own act of denial.

Thorne broke the silence at last.

"You said something yesterday," he said. "About choice."

Astrid looked up.

"You said restraint doesn't mean submission," he continued. "I believe the watchers understood that."

"I'm not sure all of them did," Astrid replied.

"No," Thorne said. "But enough."

She considered him in the firelight — the steadiness, the restraint that had once felt like a wall and now felt like a foundation.

"I don't know what the Dragon will demand," she said quietly. "But I know I won't give it something simply because it's easier."

Thorne met her gaze. "Nor should you."

She hesitated, then spoke carefully.

"When we stand before it… I need to know you won't step back out of fear of influencing me."

He didn't answer immediately.

Then: "I won't step back without your consent."

It wasn't romantic. It wasn't dramatic.

It was everything.

The land responded with a low, barely perceptible hum — agreement rendered as fact.

Later, when Astrid lay awake beneath the stars, she felt the magic within her settle into something new — not quieter, not diminished, but aligned with her will in a way that no longer felt fragile.

For the first time, she sensed the Dragon not as myth or destination, but presence — vast, patient, awake.

It knew she was coming.

And farther still, Astrid understood that the watchers were no longer wondering *if* she would break.

They were watching to see **what she would choose to become instead**.

Tomorrow, the climb would begin in earnest.

The easy paths were already behind her.

Chapter 21: The Price of the Chosen Path

The mountain did not wait for intention.

Astrid felt the shift shortly after dawn, the sensation crawling up through her feet and into her bones like cold water seeping through cracks she hadn't known were there. The land no longer hummed gently beneath her awareness. It vibrated — strained, taut, as though something had been pulled too tightly and left unable to relax.

She stopped mid — step.

Thorne noticed immediately, turning back toward her, eyes narrowing. "Is it bad?"

"It's… stressed," Astrid said, concentrating. "Not angry. Not hostile. But pushed."

The path ahead narrowed sharply, stone rising on either side like clenched teeth. The warmth she'd felt guiding them before was still there — but thinner now, stretched across unstable seams that shimmered faintly when she looked too closely.

"This isn't resistance," she murmured. "It's cost. We're walking where the land didn't expect to be altered so soon."

Thorne assessed the terrain with the practiced eye of someone who'd fought stone and cliff more times than he could count. "Can it hold?"

"Yes," Astrid said. Then, after a pause, "But not without consequence."

They proceeded carefully.

By midmorning, the trail had shifted from steep to treacherous. Loose shale slid beneath their boots. Cracks spiderwebbed across the stone, some faintly warm, others painfully cold to the touch. Each time Astrid adjusted her magic to stabilize their footing, she felt the toll — pressure building, reserves draining faster than before.

Thorne noticed.

"You're compensating," he said.

"I have to," Astrid replied. "The lattice is thin here. If I don't — "

"I know." He fell into step beside her. "Just tell me when it stops being adjustment and becomes harm."

The honesty in that made her chest tighten.

They rounded a bend where the mountain dropped sharply away into a narrow ravine. Mist clung low, obscuring depth and distance, and the air smelled metallic and sharp. Astrid flinched as the ground beneath her pulsed once — stronger than before.

Then came the sound.

Not a roar.

Not a cry.

A deep, wet tearing sound rose through the ravine, wrong in a way that made her stomach drop, followed by the grinding collapse of stone coming undone.

Astrid spun toward the edge. "That wasn't me."

"No," Thorne said grimly. "But it knows you're here."

The ravine answered with movement.

Stone peeled back in jagged sheets as something immense rose from the depths — not a construct like before, but *exposed muscle and stone fused too violently to be stable.* Veins of raw energy crackled along its surface, lightning arcing uncontrollably between fractures in its form.

This one wasn't fully formed.

This one was *breaking*.

Astrid's heart hammered painfully. "It's failing. Whatever's holding it together isn't enough."

"And is it answering you?" Thorne asked.

She closed her eyes briefly and reached — not outward, but laterally, carefully testing resonance.

"Yes," she whispered. "But it's not bound to me. It's responding to the path I stabilized — the imbalance I prevented elsewhere."

Thorne swore under his breath. "So this is the backlash."

"Yes."

The creature lurched, one massive limb shearing through stone as it dragged itself upward. A blast of raw energy erupted from its core, striking the ravine wall and sending molten fragments raining down.

They had seconds.

"Fall back?" Thorne asked.

Astrid shook her head sharply. "If it collapses without containment, it'll fracture the ravine's base. The release would destabilize half the mountainside."

Thorne stared at the creature, then back at her. "Then tell

me what you need."

Her breath hitched — not with fear, but velocity. "You anchor me," she said, fast. "Not physically. Spatially. I need a fixed reference point I can trust without pulling power into it."

His eyes locked on hers. "Tell me where."

Astrid pointed. "That rock face. It's ancient — pre-fault. If you hold there, I can calculate stabilization vectors around it."

Thorne moved without hesitation, sprinting along the ravine edge and bracing himself against the stone she'd indicated. He spread his stance, weight locked, body becoming what he had always been best at: an unmoving truth.

"I'm set," he called.

Astrid faced the creature, heart pounding as the magic surged — not wild, not uncontrolled, but *immense*. This was beyond anything she'd attempted before.

She dropped to one knee and pressed both palms to the ground.

"I won't force you," she whispered to the land. "But I won't abandon you either."

The magic rose painfully fast, pressure slamming into her chest like a held scream. She welcomed none of it — acknowledged it, named it, measured it.

The creature shrieked as the stone beneath it shifted — not collapsing, not rebelling, but *redirecting*. Astrid felt the strain tear through her shoulders, her vision blurring at the edges.

"She's failing!" Thorne shouted.

"No," Astrid gasped. "Holding — "

Too much.

The lattice buckled.

Something snapped inside her — a warning flare she had

learned to recognize too late once before.

"I can't do this alone," she cried.

Thorne's answer was immediate.

"Then don't."

He left the anchor point.

The second his weight shifted, the mountain protested violently, vibrations roaring through the ground.

"No!" Astrid shouted.

But Thorne was already moving — placing himself deliberately into the rupture zone, body interposing himself not between Astrid and the creature, but between fracture and collapse.

He spread his arms.

"Use me," he commanded. "Not the power."

Astrid screamed.

The magic surged — *responding not to command but to need* — and slammed into Thorne's presence like a wave breaking against stone. She felt the dangerous pull instantly, her power seeking to anchor too deeply, to root into him.

"No — no — " she gasped, forcing it back, redirecting with everything she had.

The land shuddered — but held.

The creature let out a fractured howl as the stone around it reconfigured — not sealing it away, but *dissolving its failing structure,* releasing the energy harmlessly into the ravine walls under Astrid's control.

With a violent crack, the thing collapsed inward, energy dispersing in a blinding flare before vanishing entirely.

Silence slammed down, brutal and absolute.

Astrid collapsed forward onto her hands, choking on air, vision darkening.

Thorne was at her side in an instant.

He knelt, hands hovering — not touching until she nodded faintly.

"I held," she whispered.

"Yes," he said fiercely. "You did."

The mountain groaned softly, fissures sealing slowly, reluctantly, but *intact*.

Astrid leaned back against the stone, shaking violently. "That cost more than I expected."

Thorne's jaw was tight. "Say how much."

She swallowed. "If I keep stabilizing things like this… the path will demand more with every step. I'll spend myself faster than I can recover."

"Then we adjust again," he said.

Tears burned unexpectedly at the corners of her eyes — not from pain, but clarity. "This is what the Dragon will see."

"Yes," Thorne said quietly. "And this is what it will answer."

Astrid lifted her gaze to the mountains rising ahead — closer now, watching.

"I won't take the Tear just to make this easier," she said.

Thorne met her eyes. "Nor should you."

"But if I don't," she continued, "then every step forward reshapes the world. I can't pretend that doesn't matter."

He nodded once. "Then the question isn't whether to choose power or restraint."

She laughed weakly. "It never was."

Night fell as they stabilized the last of the fractures, exhaustion weighing them down. When they finally made camp, Astrid pressed her hands into the earth again.

It answered — tired, but steady.

She understood with sober certainty:

The path she had chosen **would not forgive indecision**.
And the Dragon would not be waiting with mercy.
Only truth.

Chapter 22: The Measure of a Mountain

Astrid woke with the certainty of being known.

Not watched in the way the Wardens observed — not measured, not assessed — but *recognized.* The sensation rested beneath her skin like a remembered name spoken aloud, neither gentle nor cruel, simply undeniable.

She sat upright slowly, breath fogging faintly in the cold.

The mountains loomed closer now, their jagged silhouettes cutting dark against the paling sky. Even still, even unmoving, they radiated presence — vast, patient, and ancient beyond comfort. Astrid felt small in their shadow, not diminished, but placed.

Thorne noticed the shift immediately.

"You feel it too," he said quietly.

Astrid nodded. "Yes."

They didn't rush to interpret it. Some things demanded silence before understanding.

The air was different this morning — denser, as though the world itself had taken a measured breath. Stone no longer hummed lightly beneath her awareness as it had before. Instead, it *waited* — carrying weight rather than expectation.

Astrid gathered her cloak and rose, walking a few measured paces away from camp. The land did not stir in response to her movement. Her magic remained contained, alert but unprovoked.

This isn't reaction, she realized.

It's restraint.

That chilled her more than hostility would have.

The mountains ahead caught the early light, mineral veins glinting like old scars beneath stone. She pressed her palm against the ground — a habit now, but no longer an instinct born of fear.

The land answered.

Not with warmth.

Not with resistance.

But with gravity.

Astrid gasped softly as the pressure settled — gentle, enormous, impersonal. Like standing at the edge of something too large to hurry.

She drew her hand back.

Thorne approached without touching, stopping just behind her shoulder.

"It's not pushing you," he observed.

"No," Astrid said. "It's… weighing."

As if in answer, the mountain groaned.

The sound was deep and distant — not a crack or collapse, but a resonant shift that echoed through the stone beneath their feet. Pebbles rolled lazily downhill. Snow slipped from high ledges in powdery curtains.

Thorne's hand hovered near his sword. "That wasn't natural movement."

"No," Astrid agreed. "That was intentional."

The pressure intensified — not violently, but thoroughly. Astrid felt it sink into her awareness, probing not her magic, but the *way* she held it.

A presence emerged — not physically, not visually — but unmistakably.

You have come far, it seemed to say.

Astrid swallowed, pulse steady despite the enormity of it. "I haven't come far enough," she said aloud, the words trembling only slightly.

The mountain answered by shifting again.

A narrow path revealed itself two ridges higher — stone settling into form where there had been instability moments before. The way forward was not smooth, not forgiving — but it existed now.

Thorne stared. "That wasn't there yesterday."

Astrid's jaw tightened. "It's not showing us the way," she said. "It's showing me the *terms*."

They followed the path in silence, each step heavier than the last — not with exhaustion, but significance. The climb grew steeper, air thinning as altitude pressed in. Astrid's breathing remained controlled, but she felt the strain building faster now — not from lack of skill, but from scale.

Whatever tested her was patient.

And vast.

Midway up the ridge, the path ended abruptly.

Stone rose sheer before them — smooth, unbroken, ancient. No handhold, no fracture, no obvious passage.

Thorne halted. "This isn't terrain. It's a barrier."

Astrid stepped forward, heart pounding as the weight intensified once more. The air vibrated faintly, sound swallowed as if the world itself were pressing in to listen.

"This is the test," she said quietly.

She didn't reach for power immediately.

Instead, she stood before the stone and acknowledged the presence fully — not kneeling, not defiant. Simply present.

"You know why I'm here," Astrid said.

The land responded — not with words, but with memory.

A vision slammed into her — a rush of roots tearing stone, of molten veins cracking open under pressure, of mountains reshaped by arrogance and carelessness alike. She staggered, breath catching painfully.

Thorne reached for her — then stopped.

"Do you want me to anchor you?" he asked, voice steady.

Astrid nodded once. "Not yet."

The pressure deepened.

Astrid felt it then — the question beneath the weight. Not *can you*, but *will you*.

She raised her hand slowly, palm open — not toward the stone, but toward herself.

"I will not force you," she said aloud. "I won't claim what I can't carry."

The presence shifted.

The pressure sharpened — but did not retreat.

Astrid felt the strain coil tight behind her ribs. Magic stirred — stronger than it had ever been, responsive and immense — but still contained by her will.

She took one step forward.

The stone remained unmoved.

Thorne's voice came low and calm. "What is it asking?"

Astrid swallowed. "Whether I'll spend myself for passage — or endure."

The mountain creaked softly, as if amused.

Astrid closed her eyes.

"No," she said quietly. "I won't burn myself hollow just to prove I can."

She stepped back.

The air stilled.

For a heartbeat, nothing happened.

Then the stone *split.*

Not violently. Not explosively.

A seam appeared down the center of the barrier — clean, deliberate — opening slowly into a narrow pass just wide enough for a person to walk through.

Astrid exhaled shakily.

Thorne stared. "You refused."

"Yes," she said. "And it answered anyway."

The pressure eased — not vanishing, but settling into something steady and immense. Approval wasn't the right word.

Acceptance was closer.

The Dragon was not present.

But it was aware.

They made camp just beyond the pass as night fell, both of them subdued by the magnitude of what had occurred. The air here felt older — thicker with time, quieter with purpose.

Astrid sat by the fire long after Thorne had settled his gear, staring into the flames without seeing them.

"It knew," she said softly.

Thorne looked up. "Knew what?"

"That I could have pushed through." Her voice trembled slightly. "That I chose not to."

He studied her, something fierce and proud in his gaze. "That choice will matter more than power."

She nodded. "That's what frightens me."

The mountain rumbled faintly in the distance — not threatening, not aggressive. Just awake.

Astrid finally lay down, the pressure of the land still present but no longer probing.

She understood now.

The Dragon was not waiting to be impressed.

It was waiting to see what she would refuse.

And for the first time since her exile, Astrid felt ready to answer — not with submission or defiance, but with something far rarer.

Discernment.

Chapter 23: Where the Mountain Hears

The air changed as they crossed the last ridge.

Not sharply. Not violently.

But with the subtle finality of entering a place that had already decided something about them.

Astrid slowed, breath steady but heart unmistakably louder, eyes tracking the stone ahead as the mountains rose in close ranks around them. The land no longer whispered. It did not test. It simply *held* — gravity settling deeper, presence tightening like a hand closing around a truth long anticipated.

This was the near side of the Dragon's domain.

Not the lair.

The threshold.

Thorne felt it too. She could tell by the way his stride adjusted — shorter now, more deliberate — by the quiet shift of his attention from outward vigilance to inward readiness. He didn't reach for his sword. He didn't scan the cliffs.

He stayed aligned with her.

They found shelter beneath an ancient overhang scored with mineral veins that glowed faintly in Astrid's vision, colors layered so deeply they felt closer to memory than light. The stone was old enough to feel neutral — neither welcoming nor hostile.

Private.

Except Astrid knew better now.

She set her pack down slowly, palms damp against the straps.

"They're listening," she said.

Thorne nodded. "Yes."

Not the Wardens — not this time.

The attention pressing in was broader, deeper, stripped of curiosity and unburdened by urgency. It didn't peer into her magic so much as *acknowledge that it existed.*

The Dragon did not speak.

But it *attended.*

Astrid exhaled and turned, back resting lightly against the stone. "I think this is as close as we get before it expects an answer."

Thorne studied her face carefully. "Are you ready to give one?"

She hesitated.

Not from fear — but from weight.

"I don't know if I'm ready," she said honestly. "But I know I'm done delaying."

Something tightened in his expression. "Those are not the same thing."

"No," she agreed. "But they're closer than they've ever been."

The presence deepened.

Astrid felt it settle — patient, ancient, waiting.

Not for spell or submission.

For *choice.*

Her magic stirred — not demanding release, not seeking reassurance — responsive in that calm, dangerous way she had learned to respect. It wanted alignment. It wanted clarity.

She closed her eyes.

"This is the moment," she said softly. "Isn't it?"

Thorne didn't pretend otherwise. "Yes."

She opened her eyes and met his gaze.

"I need to say this out loud," Astrid said. "Not for it. For me."

He nodded. "Say it."

Astrid swallowed once, grounding herself through breath rather than earth.

"I don't want the Dragon's Tearstone because I'm afraid of what I am," she began. "And I don't want to refuse it because I'm proud. I want the choice to *mean something* beyond survival."

The weight pressed closer.

Thorne remained still, present but not intruding. She could feel him there — steady, chosen — without the need for touch.

"I don't know yet what cost I'll accept," she continued. "But I know what I won't surrender."

His voice was quiet. "Tell me."

"My agency," she said. "My timing. And the truth of what steadies me."

Her breath shook then — not from weariness, but vulnerability sharpened by scrutiny.

"That includes you," she finished.

The words settled into the stone.

The magic shifted — not surging, but deepening, aligning itself not to the presence watching them, but to the honesty she had just spoken.

Thorne felt it too. His breath caught — just slightly.

"And if the Dragon tests that?" he asked.

"Then I let it," Astrid replied. "But I won't perform denial to satisfy power."

Slowly, deliberately, she stepped closer — not touching, not closing the space entirely, but unmistakably crossing into choice.

The presence did not react.

It *observed.*

Astrid tilted her head, studying Thorne's face — a study she had postponed too long while proving herself to the world.

"I am aware," she said softly, "that choosing you here will be seen as defiance by some."

Thorne met her gaze without hesitation. "Let them misunderstand."

"That choosing restraint with you makes me appear weakened."

"It doesn't," he said firmly. "And you know that."

"Yes," Astrid agreed. "I do."

She lifted her hand halfway between them — then stopped.

The magic coiled, alert.

She looked to Thorne, silently asking without words.

"Tell me," she said quietly. "Not with instinct. With intent."

Thorne answered just as deliberately.

"I choose to stand with you," he said. "Not as shield. Not as anchor. As witness."

The presence intensified — not angrily, not approvingly — but *attentively.* The air thickened, weight pressing in a way that made Astrid keenly aware this was being *heard.*

She didn't pull her hand back.

Nor did she let it cross the final inch.

This wasn't a moment for contact.

It was a moment for *decision*.

"If choosing intimacy destabilizes me," she said, "I will wait."

"And if refusing it hollows you?" Thorne asked.

She met his gaze, resolute. "Then I will choose the version of myself that remains whole."

He nodded, something in his eyes fierce with respect.

They remained there — close, not touching, desire and restraint braided so tightly it felt structural rather than reactive. The magic within her settled into a deep, steady hum, no longer agitated by proximity or denied by caution.

The presence eased.

Astrid felt it clearly then.

Not disappointment.

Not intrusion.

Recognition.

The mountain rumbled faintly — not in threat, not in approval.

In *acknowledgment*.

She exhaled shakily. "It heard us."

"Yes," Thorne said. "And it didn't object."

Astrid laughed softly, relief and trembling pride mingling behind her ribs. "Then it knows."

"That," Thorne replied gently, "you are not coming to be measured."

She nodded. "I'm coming to decide."

They sat together as night fell, close without touching, the firelight low, the world quiet but unmistakably attentive. Astrid rested her palms against the earth — not to ask, not to shape —

— but to state her presence plainly.

She did not hide.

She did not rush.

And for the first time, beneath ancient scrutiny, Astrid felt desire and discernment align rather than compete.

Tomorrow, they would step fully into the Dragon's domain.

Tonight, she had already answered its most important question.

Chapter 24: The Gate That Breathes

The air thinned abruptly.

Not with altitude alone — but with age.

Astrid felt it the moment her boot crossed the invisible line where the stone beneath her feet shifted from merely old to *remembrance.* The ground no longer responded in tones or pressure. It *recognized.* The difference settled into her bones like a change in gravity.

She stopped.

Thorne stopped with her, not by instinct, but by agreement. They stood side by side at the edge of a wide basin carved deep into the mountain's heart. Stone arched upward on all sides, sheer and smooth in places, broken and scarred in others, as though countless attempts had been made — over lifetimes — to reshape what did not wish to be reshaped.

Heat breathed upward from below.

Not a blast. Not fire.

Breath.

Astrid swallowed.

"This is it," she said quietly.

Thorne didn't argue. The smell of sulfur and stone mingled in the air, sharp but not oppressive. The space beyond them pulsed faintly, the rhythm slow and immense — like a heartbeat too large to hurry.

The Dragon's threshold.

Not a door.

Not a lair.

A *boundary*.

They descended carefully into the basin, boots echoing softly against the stone. The further they moved, the more Astrid felt her magic retreat — not diminish, not resist, but draw inward in a way that felt instinctive.

Respectful.

"I can feel it," she murmured. "It's not suppressing me."

Thorne's voice came low and steady. "Then it's choosing not to."

They reached the center of the basin, where the stone floor sloped gently downward into darkness. Faint veins of molten light threaded the rock there — not flowing, not cooling — simply *present*, like the memory of fire held in place.

Astrid knelt.

Not in submission.

In acknowledgment.

The presence shifted.

The mountain exhaled.

Stone groaned softly beneath them as the basin changed — not collapsing, not opening fully — but *aligning*. The molten veins brightened, casting slow, rippling light across the walls, revealing ancient scorch marks and talon-scarred grooves worn deep into the rock.

A voice did not speak.

A thought did.

You come without hiding.

Astrid closed her eyes.

"Yes," she said aloud.

The pressure deepened — not crushing, but encompassing. The awareness moved through her with frightening precision, not scanning her magic, not dissecting her power, but touching the shape of her restraint, the weight of her decisions.

Thorne felt it too. His muscles tightened fractionally, not in fear, but in readiness.

Astrid breathed through the moment.

"I did not come to be absolved," she said. "And I did not come to be proven."

The presence lingered.

Then why are you here?

The question echoed — not demanding, not mocking — simply present.

Astrid opened her eyes and looked forward into the dark hollow at the basin's heart.

"Because what I carry is changing the land," she said steadily. "And I will not pretend that responsibility alone makes me worthy — or unworthy — of guidance."

Silence stretched.

Thorne remained still, not intruding, not retreating, the very picture of chosen restraint.

You refuse ease, the presence observed.

You refuse struggle as spectacle.

Astrid nodded once. "Yes."

The stone beneath them warmed — not dangerously, but noticeably.

Many come seeking a cure, the presence continued.

Few come prepared to refuse one.

Astrid's heart pounded, slow and heavy. She did not look at Thorne — but she felt him there, aligned, present, listening without claiming.

"I will not take what hollows me," she said. "And I will not prove my strength by breaking myself to fit expectation."

The mountain rumbled then — not anger, not approval.

You arrive before I summon you.

"Yes."

You arrive accompanied.

Astrid hesitated, then answered truthfully. "Yes."

For the first time, the pressure shifted — attention branching outward, touching Thorne not as obstacle or asset, but as *factor.* Astrid felt the assessment land — not judgment, but recognition of mass and choice and proximity freely given.

Thorne did not retreat.

He does not contain you, the presence observed.

He steadies.

Astrid exhaled shakily. "Yes."

Heat flared briefly — then settled.

The basin floor split slowly, stone parting with deliberate care rather than force. A descending path revealed itself — not stairs, not a ramp — but a natural slope worn smooth by ages of descent and ascent alike.

Not an invitation.

An allowance.

Thorne's gaze flicked to Astrid. "Are you ready?"

She considered the question — not strategically, not emotionally, but *honestly.*

"No," she said.

Then, after a breath: "But I'm willing."

The presence pulsed — once.

That is why you stand here.

The path waited.

Astrid rose to her feet, legs trembling not with fear but magnitude. She did not rush forward. Instead, she turned once more toward the open basin, toward the stone that had heard her.

"I will choose," she said clearly. "And you will not decide for me."

The mountain did not object.

The pressure shifted aside — like a great weight making space.

Thorne stepped closer — not touching, not claiming — but present enough that Astrid felt something steady at her shoulder without interference.

They began their descent together.

Behind them, the basin sealed — not closing them in, not cutting off retreat — but marking the threshold crossed.

The Dragon had not yet spoken.

But it had answered.

And Astrid understood with absolute clarity:

This would not be a battle of power.

It would be a reckoning of choice.

Chapter 25: The Question That Waits for Refusal

The descent ended without announcement.

Astrid felt it not when the path stopped, but when it *looped* — the sense of forward motion dissolving into a stillness so complete it felt almost unreal. The air warmed gradually, not with heat alone, but with presence pressing close enough to erase the idea of elsewhere.

The stone beneath her boots was smooth, dark, and unmarked by time.

Not untouched.

Complete.

Thorne slowed beside her, instinctively quiet, posture alert without aggression. "We're no longer approaching," he murmured. "We're… contained."

"Yes," Astrid said. "But not trapped."

The space around them was vast in shape but intimate in feel — stone curving inward into a hollow so ancient it felt less like a chamber and more like a thought given form. Veins of molten light traced the walls in lazy arcs, illuminating talon marks worn not by violence, but by repetition.

The Dragon did not appear.

It did not need to.

The presence settled like an answer arriving before its question.

You have come far, the thought resonated.

You have refused what others grasp.

Astrid inhaled slowly, grounding herself not through the earth this time — but through clarity.

"I didn't come to pass a test," she said aloud. "If that matters."

The presence paused.

It does.

The pressure shifted — not testing, not weighing — but *inviting,* like a door opening into something deeply familiar.

Images unfolded around her.

Her hands glowed steady and brilliant — not wild, not painful — magic flowing with effortless ease. Stone reshaped itself at her whim. Cracks sealed without strain. The land bent *cleanly,* answering without protest.

No backlash.

No exhaustion.

The Dragon's Tearstone shimmered at the heart of it all — warm, radiant, promising *completion.*

Astrid's breath caught painfully.

Thorne felt it the moment her pulse spiked. He didn't touch her — but his presence sharpened, ready.

"This is real," Astrid whispered. "Not illusion."

It is possibility, the Dragon's thought replied.

Stability without cost. Power without attrition.

The temptation landed exactly where it would hurt most.

She could feel it — how easy it would be. How *right* it would feel to stop measuring every breath, every choice. To let her power settle into permanence instead of vigilance.

"You would seal the lattice," the Dragon continued.

You would no longer provoke answers. The land would quiet under your hand.

Astrid stared at the vision of herself standing whole and unstrained.

"And what would I give up?" she asked.

The images shifted.

She saw herself *certain* — unquestioned, unchallenged — but alone in a way that was subtle and absolute. Others moved around her carefully, deferentially. Her power no longer required witness.

And at her side —

Thorne was absent.

Not erased.

Removed.

The presence deepened.

Your equilibrium would become internal, the Dragon observed.

You would no longer require proximity to stabilize.

Astrid's hands trembled.

"You'd cut him out of me," she said quietly.

You would be complete, the Dragon replied.

Not dependent.

Thorne spoke then — not challenging, not pleading.

"Define dependent," he said evenly.

The Dragon's attention brushed him — not hostile, not dismissive.

You are a variable, it answered.

A stabilizing influence she did not choose at birth.

Astrid's chest tightened painfully.

"But I chose him," she said.

The presence stilled.

That choice can be rendered unnecessary.

Astrid laughed softly — broken, incredulous.

"That's the temptation," she said. "Not power. Not ease." Her voice steadied. "Freedom from consequence."

The Dragon waited.

The vision pressed closer — offering certainty, silence, equilibrium that did not ask to be maintained.

Astrid stepped forward.

For a moment, Thorne's breath hitched — but he did not stop her.

She reached out —

— and then stopped herself.

Slowly, deliberately, she lowered her hand.

"No," Astrid said.

The word rang through the chamber — not defiance, not fear.

Refusal.

"I won't take a version of myself that doesn't need discernment," she continued. "Or vigilance. Or witness."

The presence did not withdraw.

It *listened.*

"I won't take power that costs me relationship," Astrid said. "Not because I'm afraid to stand alone — but because choosing connection is how I stay human."

The vision shattered.

Heat rippled outward — but did not scorch.

Then you refuse permanence, the Dragon observed.

"Yes."

You accept fluctuation.

"Yes."

You accept exhaustion.

"Yes."

And consequence.

"Yes."

Silence followed — deep and absolute.

Thorne's voice came low and steady. "Astrid."

She turned to him — not for reassurance, but confirmation.

His gaze was unwavering. "Whatever follows, you chose it cleanly."

She nodded once.

The presence expanded — not looming, not towering — but *comprehending.*

Very well, the Dragon said at last.

You may proceed.

The molten veins flared brightly, then softened, reshaping the chamber — not sealing it, not opening fully — but *reconfiguring* into something newly possible.

You will not be made safe, the thought warned.

But you will be made honest.

Astrid exhaled — a sound that felt like release after years of holding too tightly.

"That's all I wanted," she murmured.

The presence receded — not leaving, not losing interest — simply acknowledging a line crossed that could not be un — crossed.

Thorne stepped closer then — not touching, but close enough to matter.

"You refused the easy ending," he said quietly.

Astrid smiled faintly. "I refused the empty one."

The path forward opened — not glowing, not dramatic — but *allowed*.

And Astrid stepped into it knowing one thing with fierce clarity:

She had not been tested to see how strong she was.

She had been tested to see what she would protect.

Chapter 26: What Is Left Unshielded

The mountain did not close behind them.

That had been Astrid's first mistake — expecting a door to shut, a decision to be sealed with obvious finality. Instead, the passage behind remained open, its edges cooling slowly, molten veins dimming back into stone as though nothing monumental had occurred.

But something *else* had shifted.

Astrid felt it with quiet certainty as they stepped forward: the delicate buffering she had come to rely on — pressure absorbed before it reached consequence — was gone.

Not stripped away.

Withdrawn.

The air felt thinner, sharper against her lungs. Each step forward carried weight she had not noticed before, the ground no longer adjusting to her presence, no longer easing its geometry to meet her halfway.

She faltered once, barely, catching herself on instinct rather than magic.

Thorne noticed immediately.

"It's not responding," he said.

Astrid pressed her palm briefly to the rock beside her, testing.

"It is," she replied after a moment. "It's just... not helping anymore."

The words tasted strange in her mouth. Not bitterness. Acceptance.

Of course it wouldn't help.

She had refused ease.

This was the shape of that decision.

They moved on carefully, the path ahead narrower and less forgiving than anything behind them. The stone demanded attention now – slips punished, balance mattered, fatigue accumulated without mitigation.

Astrid felt every inch of it.

Her magic remained intact – alive, responsive – but it no longer preempted strain. When she used it, she *paid immediately*: heat behind the eyes, ache in the joints, breath turning shallow faster than before.

"This is different," Thorne observed quietly after she wavered again.

"Yes," Astrid said. "This is honest."

They paused at a shelf overlooking a steep drop, the world spreading vast and indifferent beneath them. Astrid leaned forward, hands on her knees, breathing carefully through the weariness threading her limbs.

"This is what it took away," she said. "The margin."

Thorne studied her closely. "And what did it leave you?"

She straightened with effort. "Choice. But no insulation from consequence."

He nodded once. "A fair trade."

Astrid laughed weakly. "You would say that."

"I mean it," he replied. "Nothing borrowed is truly yours."

They continued.

By late afternoon the strain had deepened into something that demanded management. Astrid's steps slowed, attention narrowing to placement and breath, vision sharpening with the focus that only fatigue brings.

She did not resent it.

Resentment implied expectation.

She had chosen this.

But still — her body was human.

She stumbled again, this time enough to skid against the rock. Thorne caught her instinctively, not with force, but timing — hands quick, sure, practiced.

She leaned into him without thinking.

The magic stirred sharply — then settled, realizing what this was.

Support.

Not substitution.

"Careful," Thorne murmured.

Astrid exhaled, letting herself accept the weight for one heartbeat longer than necessary before easing back upright.

"Thank you," she said quietly.

He didn't smile, didn't make it more than it was. "Anytime."

They said little after that, the climb demanding attention. The light shifted slowly toward evening, casting the stone in long shadows that seemed to stretch farther than they should.

Astrid felt it before exhaustion tipped into danger: a dull, insistent tremor beneath her ribs, warning that pushing further would invite mistakes.

She stopped.

Thorne paused at once. "You're at limit."

"Yes." She didn't argue it. "Not collapse. But precision is going."

He looked around, assessing. "We can shelter there."

He pointed to a ledge tucked beneath an overhang just wide enough to sit, protected from the wind but exposed to cold.

Astrid nodded. "It'll do."

They settled in quietly as twilight deepened, fire subdued, heat minimal. Astrid wrapped her cloak tighter, feeling the ache settle deeper into her bones now that momentum had stopped.

This was the cost.

Not crisis.

Not spectacle.

Sustainability.

Thorne watched her for a long moment, then spoke carefully.

"You don't have to prove endurance by refusing rest," he said.

Astrid met his gaze, tired but clear. "I know."

"Then why do I feel like you're holding yourself at the edge?"

She considered that, then answered honestly.

"Because this version of the path doesn't forgive complacency," she said. "And because the Dragon won't step in if I misjudge. I don't get safety nets anymore."

Thorne nodded slowly. "Then you need something else instead."

She raised an eyebrow faintly. "Which is?"

"Awareness of when to lean," he said. "Without surrendering control."

Astrid leaned back against the stone, considering the truth of that.

"I can't replace what I refused," she said quietly. "But that doesn't mean I must endure it alone."

"No," he agreed. "It means partnership becomes… infrastructure."

The phrasing struck her.

"Yes," she said. "That."

Night settled fully, stars sharp and numerous overhead. Astrid stared up at them, thinking of how many lives had made these choices unrecorded, unsupported.

She had power.

She had refused ease.

She was still allowed — perhaps required — to be human.

"That thing it took away," she said softly, "was convenience."

Thorne glanced at her. "And?"

"And it left me integrity," she finished. "And reliance that's named instead of hidden."

He nodded. "That's not weakness."

"No." Her voice was steady now. "It's risk, chosen with eyes open."

She closed her eyes then, not sleeping yet, just resting in stillness. The earth beneath them was solid — no longer adapting, no longer cushioning — but present.

She was unshielded.

And she was still standing.

The Dragon had not punished her refusal.

It had simply said:

Then walk as you are.

And Astrid understood, with steady resolve, that whatever awaited her deeper within the mountain would no longer ask whether she could choose.

It would ask whether she could **endure what she had chosen**.

Chapter 27: What the Body Needs

They did not make much distance the next day.

Astrid knew before her feet told her. The warning came from deeper in her — an inflexible heaviness that settled into muscle and breath alike, not pain exactly, but an unmistakable *no further* from a body that would obey will once or twice more and then betray it.

She stopped without apology.

Thorne halted immediately, scanning her face rather than the terrain.

"You're done," he said.

"For today," Astrid replied evenly. She waited for guilt to rise. It didn't. "If we push, I'll lose accuracy tomorrow."

Thorne nodded once, decision made. "Then we hold."

They found a shelf of stone just below the ridgeline — exposed but stable, the ground firm and unmoving beneath Astrid's palms when she tested it. No hidden hums. No warning tremors. Just solidity.

That would do.

Chapter 27: What the Body Needs

Setting camp took longer than usual.

Astrid's hands fumbled with buckles she'd managed easily days before. Her shoulders trembled faintly when she lifted her pack. The magic inside her responded to none of it — not stirring to assist, not flaring in protest. It remained quiet, letting the body carry what it could.

Thorne noticed everything. He didn't comment.

When a strap slipped from her grasp, he caught it and finished fastening the pack without looking at her, as if this were nothing more than division of labor. When she finally sat, breath uneven, he placed her water within reach without ceremony.

Only then did he speak.

"How far did you push before stopping?" he asked.

Astrid opened the flask, drank slowly, measuring. "Less than yesterday. More than I wanted."

"Holding is harder than advancing," Thorne said.

She smiled faintly. "You make that sound like doctrine."

"It is," he replied. "For guardians who survive past the first decade."

Astrid considered that, then leaned back against the stone, letting her spine rest fully for the first time in hours. The rock was cold, grounding. Good.

"Will you tell me if it gets worse?" Thorne asked quietly.

She didn't bristle at the question. That was new.

"Yes," she said. "But you'll have to trust me on *when*."

"I already do," he replied.

His certainty settled something deep and restless inside her.

The tending was unremarkable — deliberately so.

Thorne unpacked a small kit and wordlessly took her injured hand, checking the old damage first, then tracing the faint trembling in her fingers as if mapping something only he could feel. His touch was precise, impersonal, competent.

Astrid watched him work, aware of the intimacy without heat — how knowing another person's limits required closeness of a quieter kind.

"You don't need to apologize," Thorne murmured, as if reading her thoughts.

"I wasn't going to," she said.

A corner of his mouth lifted. "Good."

He wrapped the hand securely, then moved on to her shoulders, rolling stiffness out of the muscle there with steady pressure. Astrid hissed quietly, then exhaled as the ache loosened.

"That's not magic," she noted.

"No," he agreed. "This lasts."

She closed her eyes — not from pleasure, but from the relief of being handled without scrutiny.

When he stepped back, she felt the absence keenly — but she didn't chase it.

"I used to think endurance was solitary," she said after a moment.

Thorne snorted softly. "That's what people tell you when they want credit for surviving."

Astrid opened her eyes. "And you?"

"I learned early that isolation feels like strength right up until it fails," he said. "Then it kills."

She absorbed that in silence.

A simple meal followed — bland, sufficient. Astrid ate slowly, deliberately, listening to what her body asked for rather than what impatience suggested. Thorne matched her pace without comment.

Later, as the light shifted and the air cooled, Astrid attempted to stand again.

Her legs protested immediately.

She paused, recalibrated… and sat back down.

Thorne noticed but didn't speak.

After a moment, Astrid sighed once, sharp with frustration — not at herself, but at the truth.

"I don't like this part," she said.

"The stopping?"

"The needing," she corrected.

Thorne considered her from across the small fire. "Needing doesn't mean lacking."

She raised an eyebrow, unconvinced.

"It means acknowledging load limits," he continued. "Structures fail when they ignore them."

Astrid stared into the low flames, watching the way they bent with the wind rather than resisting it.

"I refused the Tear so I wouldn't hollow out," she said quietly. "I knew there would be cost. I just didn't expect it to feel this… mundane."

Thorne chuckled under his breath. "That's usually how it gets you."

She glanced at him. "And you? What does this cost you?"

He answered without hesitation. "Pace. Sleep. Attention. Sometimes fear."

Her breath caught — not sharply, but deep.

"And you're still here," she said.

"Yes."

Not because he hadn't weighed it — but because he had.

Night settled fully while they sat there, neither speaking for long stretches. The world beyond the shelter felt distant, contained. No pressure. No testing. Just waiting.

Astrid lay down carefully, arranging herself to minimize strain, aware of every soreness and limitation.

"I'll be able to move again in the morning," she said. "Slower. But clearer."

Thorne settled nearby, not too close, not far. "That's enough."

She breathed out, long and quiet.

For the first time since refusing the Tear, Astrid didn't feel the absence of what she'd declined.

She felt what remained.

A body that could rest.

A will that could choose.

A companion who did not confuse care with constraint.

Whatever lay ahead would ask more of her.

But tonight, the work was simply this:

To stop.

To let another person share the load.

To remain whole by not pretending she wasn't tired.

And that — she realized as sleep finally took her — was also a form of strength.

Chapter 28: What Remains When Nothing Is Proved

Astrid woke before the fire died.

Not abruptly. Just… aware.

The ache was still there — settled deep in bone and muscle, dull and honest — but it no longer frightened her. She lay still for a moment, listening to her breath, cataloging what answered and what did not. Her magic was present, calm, neither withdrawn nor eager.

It existed.

So did she.

Thorne sat nearby, awake, posture relaxed but attentive, gaze fixed on the eastern horizon where the sky pale-and-rose hinted at morning without quite committing to it. His presence registered before she moved, before she spoke — steady as gravity, not pulling at her, just there.

She sat up slowly.

"You didn't sleep," she said softly.

"I slept enough," Thorne replied.

Astrid nodded, accepting the truth in that without pressing for more. She drew her cloak tighter around herself, then paused when her hands shook at the movement.

Thorne noticed.

He didn't comment — just shifted closer and held the edge of the cloak while she wrapped it securely. The contact was brief, functional, but it grounded her more than she expected.

That surprised her.

"I used to think strength was loud," Astrid said after a moment. "Or visible. Something you could point to."

Thorne glanced at her, not interrupting.

"Now," she continued, "it feels quieter. Like keeping the pieces aligned long enough to rest."

He nodded once. "Endurance always looks like that from the inside."

The sky brightened incrementally, light creeping across stone that had never cared how long it waited.

Astrid leaned back against the rock, letting her shoulder brush his arm. Not testing. Not asking permission.

He didn't move away.

They sat like that for several breaths, the contact unremarked but acknowledged in the way that mattered.

"I don't regret refusing the Tear," Astrid said finally.

Thorne didn't answer immediately. When he did, his voice was careful — not doubting, but listening. "Do you regret what it took from you?"

She considered the question honestly.

"I regret the ease," she said. "I don't regret what remains."

He watched her for a long moment. "You didn't lose yourself."

"No." Her voice softened. "I gained definition."

Something eased in his expression — relief, not triumph.

"I worried," he admitted quietly, "that refusing would leave you raw. Exposed."

She smiled faintly. "It did."

"And still does?"

"Yes," she said. "But not hollow. I can feel what holds now."

She shifted slightly, turning more toward him.

"That includes you," she said plainly.

Thorne's breath slowed — not staggered, not alarmed. Just deepened, as if settling into truth rather than surprise.

"I never wanted to be a crutch," he said.

Astrid shook her head. "You aren't." She hesitated, then added, "And I don't want to pretend I don't lean."

The words stayed between them, open and unadorned.

"That doesn't make you less," Thorne said.

"I know." Her gaze held his. "It makes me *accurate*."

A quiet sound left him — not laughter, not quite. Something softer.

"I've stood next to people who needed me because they were afraid," he said. "And next to people who wanted me because they didn't want to be alone." He paused. "This… is neither."

"No," Astrid agreed. "This is what's left when nothing is proved."

She let her head rest lightly against his shoulder — not collapsing into him, not seeking shelter. Just contact. The choice was deliberate, and the magic within her responded with a subtle, pleased stillness.

Thorne didn't shift. Didn't tighten. Didn't frame the moment as anything more than it was.

His hand came up after a moment and rested between her

shoulder blades — not possessive, not tentative. Support without claim.

The land did not react.

That mattered.

Astrid closed her eyes.

"I don't know how this ends," she said quietly.

"I do," Thorne replied.

She opened her eyes, startled. "You do?"

He nodded once. "With you standing in the truth you chose."

She swallowed, emotion pressing tight behind her ribs. "That's not an ending."

"No," he said. "But it's a place to stand while the rest unfolds."

The fire crackled low beside them. Morning leaned closer.

Astrid shifted, letting herself rest there fully now — not because she couldn't sit alone, but because sitting together felt honest.

"I'm glad you stayed," she said.

Thorne didn't deflect it. "So am I."

There was no promise spoken. No vow declared.

What settled instead was something heavier and more durable.

Choice, affirmed.

Presence, maintained.

Desire, not denied — but no longer leading.

When Astrid finally stood, she did so without hurry, without apology. The weariness remained — but so did the balance.

The Dragon awaited them somewhere deeper within the mountain.

Astrid felt no need to rush toward it.

What mattered had already been acknowledged.

And whatever came next would meet them not as separate

wills orbiting crisis — but as something intact, shared, and chosen.

Chapter 29: The Judgment That Does Not Argue

The chamber did not change when the Dragon revealed itself.

That, more than anything, told Astrid she was not about to be impressed.

The space remained vast and dimly lit, stone thick with age and intention, heat breathing upward from seams deep beneath the floor. Nothing flared. Nothing shifted into spectacle. The ancient presence that had lingered as pressure and gravity simply… focused.

And then it was there.

Not appearing.

Arriving.

Astrid felt the Dragon before she saw it — an alignment of weight and awareness so immense it redefined orientation. The creature's form occupied the far end of the chamber, scales like layered stone and embered metal, wings folded tight not from submission but patience. Eyes — old beyond gender, beyond metaphor — opened fully on her.

The attention was absolute.

Thorne stiffened beside her, not moving forward, not retreating, every instinct tuned and useless all at once.

Astrid did not kneel.

She stood, spine straight, breath controlled, hands open at her sides where they trembled just slightly.

The Dragon did not remark on either choice.

You refused, it said — not aloud, not inwardly, but directly into the shared space of thought and stone.

"Yes," Astrid answered.

You were offered permanence.

"Yes."

And you walked away.

"Yes."

The Dragon's gaze did not narrow. It did not harden.

It deepened.

Most refuse because they fear the cost, it observed.

You refused because you recognized it.

Astrid swallowed, heart thudding heavy but steady.

"I won't exchange wholeness for ease," she said. "Even if the ease is deserved."

The Dragon rose then — not dramatically, not threateningly, but because conversation required scale. The heat intensified, not as punishment but inevitability, and Astrid felt her magic recoil — not suppressed, but humbled by proximity to something older than claim.

Then hear the reckoning, the Dragon said.

The ground resonated once, settling.

There will be no seal placed upon your power.

Astrid's pulse spiked.

You will continue to change the land by walking upon it.

Yes. She had expected that.

Stability will not come as a gift.

She nodded faintly.

You will fatigue.

"Yes."

You will misjudge and be required to correct.

Her jaw tightened. "Yes."

The Dragon's wings shifted, stone scraping stone in a sound that was neither approval nor threat.

Those who watch you will cease to offer restraint. They will expect authority.

Astrid inhaled, slow and deep.

And when you fail — the Dragon continued, — you will not be undone.

The words struck her harder than any danger had.

"You mean — " Her voice caught. "There's no absolution?"

There will be no erasure, the Dragon clarified.

Only accumulation.

Silence followed — vast, reverent.

The Dragon turned its gaze then — not judging, not challenging — toward Thorne.

You stand as structure, it observed.

Not as leash. Not as shield.

Thorne did not speak. Did not bow.

Your presence does not lessen her, the Dragon continued.

It permits variance.

The truth of that landed like a weight lifted — not lightness, but certainty.

This will not make her safe, the Dragon said.

But it will make her enduring.

Astrid felt something loosen behind her ribs then — not triumph, not relief, but grounded resolve.

"What happens next?" she asked.

The Dragon regarded her with an attention that was now unmistakably different.

You leave.

Astrid blinked. "That's it?"

You did not come to be kept, the Dragon replied.

You came to be recognized.

The presence shifted backward — not withdrawing, not diminishing — but releasing.

You will walk without ease.

Without certainty.

Without guarantee.

The Dragon lowered itself again, wings folding back into mass and shadow.

That is your reckoning.

Astrid exhaled slowly, feeling the weight settle — not crushing, not light.

Honest.

She turned her head slightly, enough to acknowledge Thorne without breaking stance.

"Did you hear it?" she asked quietly.

"Yes," he said.

She nodded once, then looked back to the Dragon.

"Then I will live inside that," she said. "And I will choose again as needed."

The Dragon's eyes closed — not in dismissal, but completeness.

Then go, it said.

The land knows your name now.

The pressure lifted.

The chamber did not collapse or blaze or mark her path with fire. It simply opened — stone drawing aside, pathways returning to what they had been before power tried to simplify them.

Astrid walked out without looking back.

And as the mountain sealed behind them — not trapping, not exiling — she understood the final truth of the reckoning:

The Dragon had not given her permission.

It had acknowledged her refusal as sufficient proof.

Chapter 30: What Is Carried Forward

They did not stop once they left the Dragon's domain.

Astrid noticed that first — not because she was pushed onward, but because nothing urged her to pause. There was no banner moment. No release of pressure that invited collapse or celebration. The mountain simply returned to itself, ancient and indifferent, and expected her to do the same.

The path away from the chamber was narrower than the one that had brought them down, stone worn smooth by age rather than softened by magic. Astrid placed each foot carefully, attention narrowed to the truth of gravity and balance. Her body answered. Slowly. Precisely. It did not offer enthusiasm.

That was fine.

Thorne moved beside her without comment, pace adjusted half a breath at a time until it matched hers. Not guiding. Not urging. Just *there,* occupying the same rhythm.

She felt the absence before she thought to name it.

It was not silence. The mountain still breathed. Heat still rose faintly through the soles of her boots. But the vast, directive presence — the one that had watched, weighed, corrected — had withdrawn entirely.

The Dragon no longer listened.

Not because it was displeased.

Because it was finished.

Astrid's magic stirred once, lightly, as if to confirm this, then settled back into itself. No buffering folded around her awareness. No smoothing of sharp edges. When a rock shifted underfoot, it stayed shifted. When her breath hitched from strain, it remained hers to manage.

She stumbled once.

Not a fall — just a slip of attention that sent pebbles skittering into the darkness below. Thorne's hand came out instantly, not grabbing, but halting momentum just long enough for her to find her center again.

She nodded. He let go.

No comment passed between them.

That silence mattered.

They descended in stages. When Astrid felt the warning tremor beneath her ribs — the one that warned of future inaccuracy rather than immediate danger — she stopped. Thorne stopped too, already looking at her face instead of the path.

"Here?" he asked.

She pressed her palm to the rock at her side, checking — not for magic, but for reliability. The stone was cold. Solid. Utterly unimpressed by her presence.

"Yes," she said. "If we go farther tonight, I'll compensate instead of choose."

That cost was no longer theoretical. She understood it too clearly now.

Thorne inclined his head once. "Then we camp."

Setting things down was slower work than before.

Astrid's fingers were clumsy — not weak, simply overspent. The buckle of her pack caught twice before she breathed, slowed, and refastened it with deliberate attention. She felt the ache along her forearms where magic had burned shallow channels of fatigue into flesh.

No glow remained.

No echo of the Dragon's presence lingered.

Just consequence.

Thorne noticed everything and fixed nothing unless asked.

When she sat, he passed her water. When she stood again and faltered, he matched her weight until balance returned. The tending was subtle, unromantic, and profoundly intimate in a way no declaration could rival.

The fire burned low. They didn't coax it higher.

Astrid sat cross-legged near its edge, palms extended briefly to warm, then withdrawn. Her magic did not join the gesture. It rested inside her like a muscle now — willing, unexalted, resolutely honest.

She exhaled.

"This feels… smaller," she said.

Thorne glanced up from his inspection of a cracked strap. "Tell me how."

"The Dragon didn't take anything," Astrid said slowly. "But it stopped *carrying* parts of it for me."

"Yes."

"So everything has scale again," she continued. "Not meaning — effort."

Thorne considered that. "That's usually how reality behaves."

She huffed a quiet breath of laughter. "I liked it better when it bent."

"And you knew that liking it was the danger," he replied.

She nodded, gaze fixed on the low flames. "I thought refusal would feel like loss."

"And?"

"It feels like standing alone in bad weather," she said. "Cold. Clear. Possible."

The night deepened around them. No watcher stirred. No test surfaced. The mountain was finished with surface lessons.

Later, when Astrid shifted to lie down, her knee protested sharply. She hissed, then laughed once — more tired than amused.

Thorne crouched nearby instantly. "That's new."

"It's not injury," she said after a moment, probing sensation carefully. "Just tomorrow arriving early."

She flexed the joint slowly, felt the grind ease.

"You could smooth it," Thorne said, not suggesting — just acknowledging the option.

Astrid shook her head. "If I start smoothing every edge, I'll forget which ones matter."

He respected that without further comment.

She lay back fully then, pressing her spine to the stone, eyes fixed on the narrow strip of stars visible between cliffs. They looked unchanged — distant, patient, unknowable.

"Did you expect it to feel like this?" she asked quietly.

Thorne folded himself down near her — close enough to share warmth, far enough to remain separate. "No."

"What did you expect?"

He was silent for several breaths. "Relief," he admitted. "Or devastation."

"And instead?"

"Integration," he said. "Which is harder to name."

She smiled faintly at the word.

"I don't feel finished," she said.

"No," Thorne agreed. "But you feel continuous."

That settled something deep and restless in her.

Before sleep took her, Astrid reached one hand out — not searching, not grasping — and rested it lightly over his wrist where it lay near the fire.

The contact was gentle. Deliberate. Chosen.

Her magic stirred once, pleased but quiet.

Nothing else answered.

This — she realized as her breath evened — was what she had refused the Tear for.

Not grandeur.

Not certainty.

But the ability to remain herself from one moment to the next without erasure.

Whatever came next would not simplify.

But it would *connect*.

And that was enough to walk with.

Chapter 31: How They Stand

They did not leave the mountain that night.

Astrid realized that first — not as an instruction, not as resistance from the land, but as a simple truth that settled into her bones the moment her feet carried her beyond the Dragon's threshold. The path remained open. The stone gave no warning. The air did not harden or thin.

She was simply… done.

Not finished.

But complete for the moment.

They found shelter not far below the upper passages, where the mountain's weight softened just enough to allow rest without invitation. A shallow shelf curved inward, stone worn smooth by centuries of melt and freeze. It was exposed to the sky but guarded against wind. Old heat lingered there, faint as memory.

Thorne set their packs down without comment.

Astrid stood a few paces away and breathed.

Her magic lay inside her differently now. Still present. Still responsive. But where once it had pressed at the edges of thought — eager, unstable — it now rested deeper, heavier, like a muscle after strain rather than a storm waiting to break.

Nothing feels lighter, she thought.

She knelt slowly and pressed her palm against the stone.

Not to draw.

Not to test.

Just to check.

The contact was clear and immediate — and restrained. The earth acknowledged her presence without reaching back, without leaning toward her intent. No buffering warmth wrapped her awareness. No subtle adjustment smoothed the uneven places beneath her touch.

The land did not help.

It simply remained.

Astrid inhaled sharply and withdrew her hand.

Behind her, Thorne watched.

He did not ask what she felt.

He did not step closer.

He trusted her to speak when she was ready.

They built a small fire with efficient care. Thorne coaxed the flame low and steady, careful not to draw more heat than necessary. Astrid watched the process with a focus she had once reserved for spellwork, aware now of how small choices conserved energy rather than spent it.

They ate in silence — simple food, nothing ceremonial. The act itself felt important for its ordinariness.

Afterward, Astrid wrapped her cloak tighter around herself and settled near the fire. She could feel fatigue threading through her limbs in a way that was unmistakably physical. No magical buffer delayed it. No instinct rose to dull it.

This exhaustion was hers.

She leaned back against the stone and closed her eyes.

Thorne added his blanket without a word — folded carefully around her shoulders rather than draped, leaving her hands free and her posture unchanged. The contact was brief, intentional.

"Thank you," she said quietly.

He nodded and resumed his watch, positioning himself between her and the open slope without crowding her space.

For a long while, nothing happened.

No watchers appeared.

No tremor rippled beneath their feet.

The mountain slept.

Astrid opened her eyes and stared into the fire, watching the way the flame bent and straightened with the shift of air.

"I checked," she said eventually.

Thorne's gaze moved to her — not startled, not invasive. Present.

"And?" he asked.

"My magic is still there," she said. "But it isn't cushioning anything anymore."

He considered that. "No margin."

"No," she agreed. "No delay. No forgiveness built in."

She flexed her fingers slowly, feeling the residual ache in her hands, the honest consequences of strain.

"I know now what I gave up," she continued. Her voice was steady, but thin in the way truths sometimes were. "The Tear wasn't just permanence. It was insulation."

Thorne's jaw tightened slightly. "And you refused it anyway."

"Yes."

The fire popped softly.

Astrid drew in a breath and let it out.

"Nothing feels lighter," she said. "But it feels cleaner."

That was the truth of it. Not relief. Not triumph.

Clarity.

Thorne angled his head slightly, eyes still on the dark beyond the firelight. "And the cost?"

She didn't answer immediately.

She pressed her palm once more to the stone beside her — careful, deliberate — and listened.

"When I overreach," she said slowly, "I'll feel it immediately. When I misjudge, there won't be time for the land to correct me." Her throat tightened faintly. "I'll have to stop on my own. Rest on my own. Ask."

Thorne shifted then — not closer, not farther. Simply marking the weight of the admission.

"And," Astrid added quietly, "I won't be able to pretend endurance is noble when it's just avoidance."

He nodded once. "That was always a lie the strong were told."

She smiled faintly at that.

The wind moved across the stone above them, carrying snow dusted fine as ash. Thorne adjusted his stance subtly, blocking the draft's edge before it could steal warmth from her side of the fire.

Astrid noticed.

She always did.

She leaned back more fully against the rock, blanket drawn close — not to hide, but to steady.

"Will you sleep?" Thorne asked quietly.

"In a little while," she said. "I want to feel this first."

He understood.

She closed her eyes again and let awareness expand — not outward, not searching — but inward.

Her magic responded...but only as much as she let it.

It warmed her core faintly, then stopped.

No surge followed. No hunger.

That, more than anything, told her what had changed.

"When I touch it now," she murmured, "it doesn't try to finish the thought for me."

Thorne exhaled slowly. "Good."

"Yes," she agreed. "Terrifying. But good."

Silence returned.

Eventually, Astrid shifted, joints protesting in an honest way that made her wince. Thorne noticed at once and moved — not to help, but to give her something to brace against as she adjusted her position.

She accepted the support without comment.

They settled then — side by side without touching, close enough that warmth passed between them without effort. Thorne remained awake, posture relaxed but vigilant, gaze scanning the darkness beyond the firelight.

Astrid watched him for a time.

"You didn't interfere," she said quietly.

"I didn't need to," he replied.

"Earlier," she continued, "before the Dragon... I think part of me believed you were meant to shield me from consequence."

His attention sharpened, but he didn't interrupt.

"I know now that would have hollowed this choice," she went on. "If the cost had been absorbed by someone else."

"Yes," Thorne said. "That's why I waited."

She nodded slowly. "Thank you... for not saving me from it."

His voice was low, steady. "You didn't ask to be spared."

The fire burned lower. Thorne fed it just enough to last the night.

Astrid shifted onto her side, drawing the blanket closer. She was aware now not only of fatigue, but of safety — the kind that didn't rely on wards or power, just presence and attention.

"Sleep," Thorne said softly.

"I will," she replied. "Soon."

She paused, then added, "Stay close."

He didn't hesitate. He reached out and anchored the blanket more securely around her shoulders — not holding her, not trapping heat, just ensuring it wouldn't slip.

"I'm here," he said.

Astrid closed her eyes.

The mountain did not stir.

No voice spoke.

No power tested her resolve.

What remained was exactly what she had chosen: effort without distortion, intimacy without obligation, and a path that would ask her to decide again tomorrow, and the day after that, and the day after that.

Thorne kept watch as night deepened, guarding sleep not because she demanded it, but because it mattered.

And when Astrid finally drifted into rest, her magic stayed quiet — not diminished, not bent.

Simply hers.

Chapter 32: What Is Tended

Morning did not announce itself.

It arrived gently, as if the world had decided Astrid deserved transition rather than demand. The air warmed by degrees rather than moments. The light shifted from slate to pearl without glare. Even the mountain seemed content to let shadow loosen at its own pace.

Astrid woke aware of every joint.

Not pain — yet — but the clear inventory of effort made and paid for. Her shoulders held a quiet ache. Her thighs complained when she shifted. The hand she had injured days before was stiff in a way that suggested weather-remembered injuries better than people did.

She did not reach for her magic.

She lay still and breathed instead, counting the steady rhythm of inhalation and release. Her magic lay present beneath that breath, contained and patient. It did not press at the edges of her awareness. It did not anticipate.

It waited.

That alone would have unnerved her once.

Now, it felt honest.

She sat up slowly, bracing one palm against the stone behind her. The rock was cool and unyielding — not hostile, not supportive. Simply there.

Thorne was awake already.

He sat near the edge of their small camp, cloak folded beside him, forearms resting on his knees. His posture was relaxed but alert in the way of someone who understood vigilance not as anxiety, but as attentiveness. He did not look at her immediately.

He trusted her to say something if she needed to.

Astrid noticed that before anything else.

"Good morning," she said quietly.

Thorne inclined his head. "You slept."

"Yes," she replied, then amended softly, "I rested."

That earned the faintest curve of his mouth.

"How does it feel?" he asked.

Astrid checked herself carefully — not out of suspicion, but respect.

"Tired," she said after a moment. "But not brittle."

He nodded. "That's workable."

They did not rush.

There was no reason to.

Breakfast was utilitarian. Bread softened with water, a dried apple shared without ceremony, tea warmed gently rather than brewed strong. Astrid noticed, watching Thorne's movements, how deliberately he avoided excess — how everything about his presence aimed at sustainability rather than performance.

"You do this instinctively," she said.

Thorne glanced up. "Do what?"

"Resource management," Astrid replied. "Energy. Heat. Motion."

He considered that. "It's easier to keep going if you never borrow from tomorrow."

The phrasing lodged somewhere deep in her chest.

After they ate, Astrid stood — and immediately regretted it. Her knees protested sharply, the ground seeming farther away than it should have been. She stiffened, not wanting to draw attention.

Thorne noticed anyway.

"Sit," he said — not command, not concern. Just plain directive.

Astrid hesitated for half a breath, reflex and stubbornness warring.

Then she sat.

The relief was immediate and humbling.

"That," she said dryly, "is going to take getting used to."

"Yes," Thorne agreed. "Especially for people raised to mistake endurance for virtue."

Astrid snorted softly. "Demetra blesses growth," she said. "Not depletion. We just forget that when failure scares us."

They stayed where they were long enough that the morning truly arrived.

Birdsong filtered tentatively down the slopes. Frost retreated from shaded stone in reluctant beads. The world felt… calm.

Not safe.

Just calm.

Astrid flexed her injured hand carefully, rotating her wrist, testing range of motion rather than strength. The ache sharpened, then softened as blood moved.

"You can rewrap that," Thorne said.

"I know." She glanced at him. "Will you hand me the kit?"

He did so without comment, his movements easy and unintrusive. Astrid took the time she needed — cleaning the skin, resetting the wrap with more care than before. She was aware of Thorne watching, not with scrutiny, but attentiveness.

"Does it bother you?" she asked quietly.

"What?"

"Seeing control look like this instead of spectacle."

Thorne considered her question seriously.

"No," he said. "It reassures me."

"Why?"

"Because spectacle breaks first," he replied. "This doesn't."

They spent the next hours doing very little.

That was the point.

Astrid walked the perimeter of their small clearing slowly, grounding herself through motion alone. She practiced lifting small stones and setting them back down — not to train power, but to reassure herself she could still engage without escalation. The magic obeyed.

Then quieted when she stopped.

Thorne did not interfere. He repaired gear. He reorganized packs. He stood watch when needed and sat when it didn't.

At one point, Astrid misjudged her footing and stumbled — not enough to fall, but enough to wobble. Thorne moved without thinking, steadying her elbow for a single moment before releasing her again.

They froze.

Not from danger.

From awareness.

Astrid felt the magic stir sharply, then slow — responding not to panic, not to desire, but to precision. She breathed through it deliberately.

"Okay," she murmured.

"Yes," Thorne said quietly.

He did not pull away in panic. He did not hold on longer than necessary.

That mattered more than either of them said aloud.

Later, when the sun sat higher, Astrid lowered herself onto a flat slab of stone and leaned back, exhaustion settling into her limbs in a way that felt earned rather than alarming.

"This is the part clerics don't teach," she said.

"Which part?"

"The waiting," she replied. "The tending. They focus on invocation and intervention. Not recovery."

Thorne sat nearby, one knee drawn up, gaze on the horizon. "Recovery doesn't make good stories."

"No," Astrid agreed. "But it makes survival."

She breathed out slowly, eyelids lowering.

"Stay," she said.

Thorne didn't move closer.

"I am," he replied.

Silence followed — not awkward, not heavy. Simply shared.

Astrid knew, distantly, that readers loved danger. Loved climaxes and revelations and dramatic turning points.

But this — this quiet, unglamorous honesty — felt like the truest testament to what she and Thorne were actually building.

Not romance as consumption.

Romance as *infrastructure*.

As the afternoon cooled, clouds drifted in, not threatening

weather, just dulling the light. Astrid stirred, wincing faintly as she shifted.

"Before," she said slowly, "I would have used magic to smooth that."

Thorne didn't respond immediately.

"And I would've told myself that meant efficiency rather than avoidance."

"Yes," he said finally.

She frowned slightly. "You sound… relieved."

"I am," he admitted. "If you'd kept smoothing edges, I would've started worrying about when you'd stop noticing them."

Astrid considered that.

"Does that make me harder to walk beside?" she asked.

"It makes you honest," Thorne replied. "Which is easier."

The answer threaded through her in unexpected ways.

They tended the fire together that evening — not out of need, but ritual. Astrid noticed how deliberate Thorne's spacing was, how clearly he marked where heat belonged and where it did not. She mirrored his care without being asked.

"How long has it been since you rested like this?" she asked quietly.

"Long enough to forget it was allowed," he said.

She smiled faintly. "Then let this count."

It did.

When night settled, it did so gently. No watchers appeared. No sudden caution prickled at Astrid's awareness. The land felt… neutral again.

Not indifferent.

Just not invested.

Astrid lay back beneath her cloak, tension finally draining

from places she'd been guarding unconsciously. Her magic sank deeper, as if acknowledging that no immediate choice was required.

"Thorne," she said drowsily.

"Yes?"

"If someone looks at this — at us — and thinks it's hesitation..."

"They're wrong," he said immediately.

"And if they think restraint means fear?"

"They misunderstand," he replied. "And misunderstanding is not your responsibility to correct."

She exhaled, something fragile and tight loosening behind her ribs.

"I'm glad you're here," she said simply.

Thorne did not respond right away.

Then: "So am I."

He kept watch through the night — not because threat demanded it, but because care did. Astrid slept more deeply than she had in weeks, body given permission to repair rather than brace.

No dreams haunted her.

No power exposed itself.

When morning came again, it did so quietly.

And Astrid woke knowing, with steady clarity:

This was what let a story go on.

Chapter 33: How the World Holds Them

They reentered the world quietly.

Astrid noticed it first in what did *not* happen.

No pull twisted beneath her ribs as they descended into gentler land. No unconscious smoothing followed her steps. The air did not thicken around her, nor did stone lean closer beneath her boots. The world resumed itself without commentary, as if her passage were simply one more fact among many.

That absence felt heavier than any attention.

They came down out of the mountains by an old service track — stone-packed but broken along the margins, the kind of road maintained only when something went wrong badly enough to demand repair. Moss crept across its edges in stubborn seams. Small flowers bowed low where soil had managed to gather in the cracks.

Astrid walked carefully, testing pace rather than ground. Her body answered honestly. Fatigue pressed, but did not threaten collapse. Her magic remained present and quiet, no longer triangulating every step, no longer buffer or interpreter.

It waited.

Thorne adjusted naturally to her tempo without remark, shortening his stride, easing his weight back on steeper descent. It wasn't the sort of accommodation people noticed unless they were watching carefully — and Astrid knew by now that most people didn't.

They reached lower territory shortly before midday.

The first sign of habitation was smell rather than sound: woodsmoke tangled with damp earth and the faint sweetness of something baking too long. The second sign was fencing — old timber reinforced with stone, practical rather than elegant.

Astrid slowed instinctively.

The last time she had walked openly among people, she had been a known quantity — or a feared one.

Now, she was neither.

A woman paused at the fence as they passed, hands stilling in the work of tying bundles of cut grass. Her gaze flicked to Thorne, then to Astrid. Curious. Measuring. Not alarmed.

Good, Astrid thought. Neutral.

They continued past without exchange.

A little farther on, the road widened into something like a crossing — three tracks meeting at a juncture marked by a stone pillar with no inscription left on it anymore. The base had been smoothed by generations of hands, not reverent, just practical.

Two traders stood there, debating direction in low voices. One glanced up as Astrid and Thorne approached.

"Road's washed out east," the trader said to them conversationally, like an offering rather than a warning. "North's better if you're light."

Thorne inclined his head. "Thank you."

"No trouble." The trader hesitated, then added, "Mountains been restless lately."

Astrid felt the tiniest stir in her magic — not reaction, just recognition.

"Yes," she said simply. "They have."

The trader nodded, satisfied, and turned back to his companion.

They moved on.

Astrid let her breath out slowly.

"That was... normal," she observed.

"Yes," Thorne replied.

"I should feel relieved."

"And?"

"And I don't," she admitted. "I feel... visible."

Thorne glanced sideways at her. "Those are not the same thing."

"No," she agreed. "But I think they touch."

They found a place to rest near a shallow stream, its banks packed with smooth river stone worn pale by time and weather. Astrid knelt and washed her hands, grounding herself through the physical ritual rather than intent. The water ran cold and clear. The world responded with nothing more than reflection.

Behind her, Thorne took watch without theatrics. He didn't posture. He simply occupied space in a way that implied it was his to guard.

Astrid noticed a young traveler on the opposite bank pause, glance, then continue. No fear. No recognition. Just assessment and decision.

She straightened slowly.

"It's strange," she said. "To be this... ordinary."

Thorne smiled faintly. "Give it time. You'll remember why people fight so hard to stay that way."

They spent the afternoon moving slowly, letting Astrid's stamina — not ambition — determine distance. By the time the road curved gently toward cultivated land, her knees ached in that dull way that implied rest would be wise later rather than immediately.

A small settlement took shape ahead — not really a village, more a clustering of purpose: a low inn with smoke curling from its chimney, a stable that leaned too far to the left and had given up correcting itself, a well worn smooth by palms rather than pulley.

Astrid halted.

Thorne stopped with her, waiting.

"I want to go through," she said. "Not around."

He studied her carefully, not for capability but consent. "Then we will."

They entered without announcement.

A few heads turned. Most did not. Someone called from inside the inn, voice lifted in irritation or familiarity — hard to tell which. Life continued.

Astrid felt it then: not pressure, not warning, but something like remembered expectation.

This was what the world looked like when it was not shaping itself around her.

The innkeeper — a broad-shouldered figure with flour dusting their sleeves — looked up as Astrid and Thorne crossed the threshold. Their gaze flicked between Astrid's travel-stained cloak and Thorne's size, lingering just long enough to scrape curiosity.

"Rooms?" the innkeeper asked.

"Food," Astrid said first — voice steady, unaugmented. "And water."

The innkeeper nodded. "We've got stew. Bread's fresh enough if you're forgiving."

Astrid smiled faintly. "I am."

They took a table near the wall, wood polished smooth by years of elbows and unremarkable conversations. Astrid sat first, careful of her knees. Thorne sat across from her, posture relaxed without inviting attention.

When the bowl arrived, Astrid breathed in the steam — root vegetables, too much salt, something smoky beneath it all.

Ordinary.

Her magic did not react. Did not stir.

She ate slowly, savoring texture rather than novelty.

Across from her, Thorne ate with practiced efficiency that softened slightly as he noticed her pace and matched it.

That, too, felt deliberately chosen.

Halfway through the meal, Astrid realized she was being watched.

Not casually.

The attention came from the bar — someone seated alone, posture relaxed but gaze intent. Not hostile. Intentional.

Astrid glanced briefly, then away.

"Do you feel that?" she asked quietly.

"Yes," Thorne replied.

"Watcher?"

"Observer," he said. "Different posture."

Astrid nodded.

After a moment, the person rose and approached — not

intruding, not hesitant. They stopped at a respectful distance.

"Forgive me," they said. "May I speak plainly?"

Astrid tilted her head. "You are."

The observer's mouth twitched faintly. "You walk like someone who knows when not to push."

Astrid's fingers stilled.

"Once," she said carefully, "I walked like someone who thought pushing was the answer."

The observer inclined their head. "I thought so."

Thorne did not move.

"And now?" the observer asked.

Astrid met their gaze steadily. "Now I rest when I must."

A pause.

"Good," the observer said. "That's rarer."

They stepped back without further comment and returned to their seat.

Astrid exhaled slowly.

"That's new," she murmured.

"Yes," Thorne agreed. "You're being read for restraint instead of power."

She considered that as she finished her meal.

They left the inn before dusk, choosing not to linger. Camp was made beyond the settlement in a stand of trees that smelled faintly of resin and last year's rain.

Astrid lowered herself onto her bedroll with more gratitude than pride.

"I feel like I should say something declarative," she said tiredly. "About us. About what this means."

Thorne shook his head slightly. "You don't."

"Why?"

"Because what you're doing is louder," he replied.

She let that sit.

The fire burned low between them — not because of scarcity, but respect for evening. Astrid rested her hands against the earth, not to ground, but to acknowledge.

No response came.

That absence felt earned.

"Thorne," she said quietly.

"Yes?"

"When this becomes harder — and it will — "

"I know," he said.

" — I don't want you to pre-empt my choice by stepping back."

He met her gaze. "I won't."

"And I won't pre-empt yours by clinging."

His mouth curved with something like approval. "That's balance."

Astrid leaned back and looked up at the sky threading itself into visibility. She felt weary and grounded and deeply unfinished.

It felt right.

They slept without incident.

No eyes pressed at the edge of awareness. No land stirred beneath them.

When Astrid woke before dawn, she turned on her side and found Thorne already awake, gaze lifted toward the faintest light at the horizon.

She rested her forearm lightly against his without ceremony.

Either of them could have moved away.

Neither did.

The world, upon being offered nothing dramatic, accepted that too.

They would move on soon.

But for now, this — this quiet maintenance of choice and presence — was enough.

✦✦✦

Astrid lay awake longer than she expected.

The fire burned low, fed just enough to keep the night from pressing too close. Wind moved gently through the trees, carrying the sound of distant water and something quieter beneath it — the rhythm of a world unconcerned with her decisions, even as those decisions reshaped how she existed within it.

Her body ached in honest places.

She welcomed the sensation. It anchored her to herself in a way magic never could.

Thorne sat nearby, watch half-kept, posture loose but attentive. He did not pace. He did not sharpen steel simply to fill the silence. He existed in that particular stillness reserved for someone fully present but not pressing.

Astrid studied the shape of him in the low light — not with hunger exactly, not with fantasy — but with awareness sharpened by rest and truth.

Earlier in the journey, she had noticed him the way one noticed terrain: obstacle, shelter, orientation point.

Now she noticed him the way one noticed gravity.

Not dominating.

Constant.

It startled her how much that recognition unsettled and steadied her at the same time.

She turned onto her side, breath quiet, magic dormant but aware.

"Thorne," she said softly.

"Yes," he replied at once, no trace of sleep in his voice.

"I've been thinking about what it means that the land doesn't lean toward me anymore."

He waited.

"It means," she continued slowly, "that every step forward carries its full weight. There's no advance grace. No softening before consequence."

"That's true," he said.

She swallowed. "It also means that if I move toward something now — toward *someone* — nothing will intervene to decide for me."

Thorne's breath changed — not sharply, but noticeably.

"That," he said carefully, "sounds like clarity."

"It feels like risk," Astrid replied.

"And yet," he said, "you aren't retreating."

"No," she agreed. "Because this isn't fear."

Silence stretched, alive but not tense.

"I'm aware," she said after a moment, "that what I'm choosing right now is not neutral."

Thorne shifted slightly so he faced her — not looming, not closing distance. Just aligned.

"Tell me what you mean."

"I mean," Astrid said, choosing her words with care, "that restraint can become another way of hiding if it isn't named."

"Yes."

"And that pacing only works if it acknowledges where it's going."

Thorne's gaze held hers, steady and intent. "And where is it going?"

Astrid's chest tightened — not with panic, but precision.

She did not look away.

"Forward," she said.

The word settled between them — not as promise, not as demand. As direction.

Thorne exhaled slowly. "Good."

She searched his face, found no surprise there. No defensive withdrawal. No need to frame her words as premature or dangerous.

"I don't want the future to happen to me," Astrid continued. "I want to meet it intact."

"And you intend to," Thorne replied.

"Yes." Her voice softened, though her resolve did not. "That includes not pretending this doesn't exist."

She gestured gently at the space between them.

Thorne considered her for a long moment.

"You're not asking me to wait without context," he said.

"No."

"You're not saying 'not ever.'"

"No."

"And you're not asking me to decide for you."

Astrid's throat tightened. "Never."

A quiet understanding settled — heavy, durable.

Thorne nodded once. "Then understand this."

She focused on him fully now.

"I'm not interpreting what you're doing as hesitation," he said. "And I'm not planning an end point where patience breaks into impulse."

Something loosened behind her ribs.

"You're saying — "

"I'm saying," Thorne replied, "that when you decide to step across that line, it won't surprise me. And it won't frighten me."

Astrid closed her eyes briefly.

That mattered more than she had expected.

"When that moment comes," she said quietly, "I don't want it to carry the weight of being overdue."

"It won't," Thorne said. "It will carry the weight of being chosen."

She breathed that in, slow and deep.

The magic inside her stirred faintly — not reacting, not warning. Accepting.

Astrid looked at him again.

"There will come a point," she said, "when choosing not to act will cost more than acting."

"Yes," Thorne agreed without hesitation.

"And when that point arrives — "

"I will not rush you," he said.

"And you won't retreat from it either."

"No."

The word fell with certainty.

They sat there a long while after that, the silence doing no violence to what had been said.

Astrid let herself imagine — not detail, not outcome — but inevitability without urgency.

Her awareness of Thorne was physical now, not just conceptual. She could sense the warmth he radiated, the steadiness of his breathing, the quiet restraint he held like another oath alongside guarding and watch.

And beneath that awareness lived want.

Clear.

Undeniable.

Patient.

She did not suppress it.

She acknowledged it as she would weather at the horizon — approaching, uncompromising, not yet arrived.

"This is harder than denial," she admitted.

"Yes," Thorne said. "Because it asks for presence."

She smiled faintly. "And presence doesn't distract."

"No," he agreed. "It intensifies."

Astrid leaned back onto her bedroll, eyes on the dark sky above the trees. Stars threaded themselves into sight as the night deepened, sharp and immutable.

"I used to think desire was a force to be managed," she said. "Like magic gone wrong."

"And now?"

"Now I think it's information," she replied. "About what matters enough to demand responsibility."

Thorne's voice was low. "That's dangerous knowledge."

"Yes."

She turned her head just enough that her shoulder brushed his knee.

The contact was light. Intentional. Chosen.

Neither of them moved away.

The magic remained still.

Astrid smiled to herself.

She had feared that choosing control would mean choosing absence.

Instead, it had clarified shape.

She knew — without doubt — that when she finally allowed herself to cross that line, it would not dissolve her discipline or fracture her sense of self.

It would deepen it.

Not because restraint had starved her.

But because it had taught her how to arrive intact.

Whatever came next would not arrive in secret.

It would not arrive in desperation.

And it would not arrive alone.

That knowledge settled into her bones more securely than any promise.

When Astrid finally slept, it was without tension coiled beneath her ribs — without magic poised to intervene, without fear of what waited.

Only awareness.

Only direction.

Only the sure knowledge that the fire she had not yet touched was real —

and that choosing when to reach for it was its own kind of strength.

Epilogue: What Continues

They did not announce themselves.

When Astrid and Thorne crossed out of the high foothills and into lands shaped by people as much as weather, the world did not shudder or reorient itself. Roads stayed roads. Fences remained where they had been hammered into place. Smoke rose from chimneys in slow, domestic spirals.

Astrid noticed the absence immediately.

Once, the land had leaned toward her decisions — stone listening too closely, roots responding before she touched them. Now it did not anticipate. It did not soften its geometry or brace itself in advance.

It waited.

That difference felt earned.

They followed a trade road for half a day without incident. Travelers passed them without stopping, eyes lingering for reasons that had nothing to do with power at first glance: Thorne's size, Astrid's posture, the way they walked with an unspoken agreement that required neither explanation nor correction.

By afternoon, Astrid felt it — the familiar prickle at the edge of awareness that no longer meant danger, only acknowledgment.

"We're not invisible," she said quietly.

Thorne didn't look back. "Did you want to be?"

She shook her head. "No. I just wanted to notice."

They stopped near a stream that ran steady and shallow, edging a small green basin beaten smooth by regular use. Someone had stacked stones there once, long ago, but time and weather had pulled them apart again.

Astrid crouched and washed her hands in the cold water, grounding herself through ritual rather than necessity. Her magic stirred faintly — responsive, contained, patient.

Still unfinished.

She straightened and found three figures standing at a respectful distance.

Wardens.

Different ones than before.

They did not step into the basin. They did not speak first.

Astrid took in the set of them — how deliberately neutral they were, how carefully *uncertain*. No measuring pressure slid across her awareness. No attempt was made to provoke response or reaction.

Good, she thought. They listen better now.

One inclined their head. "Daughter of the Altered Path."

Astrid did not correct the title.

"You've been recognized," the Warden continued. "That status will invite interpretation."

Astrid let her hands fall loosely at her sides. "That's unavoidable."

"And alignment?" another asked. "Do you travel under sanction?"

Astrid glanced briefly at Thorne — just long enough to confirm what she was about to say — and then answered.

"I travel under choice," she said. "Mine."

Silence followed — not awkward, just deliberate.

"And the Guardian?" the first Warden asked.

Thorne's voice was calm and unforced. "I walk beside her until one of us decides otherwise."

Astrid felt her magic settle at the phrasing — not surging, not reacting. Accepting.

The Wardens withdrew without further challenge.

As they vanished back into the terrain, Astrid felt something loosen — an old expectation finally released.

"They didn't ask what I intended to do," she said.

"No," Thorne agreed. "They asked whether you were contained."

She smiled faintly. "And accepted the answer."

They made camp that evening not far from the road, close enough to hear the faint sounds of other travelers settling for the night. Laughing voices carried briefly and faded. Someone argued quietly over firewood. Life went on without reference to her.

Astrid liked that more than she had expected.

Later, as dusk deepened and the fire burned low, she sat with her knees drawn up, cloak wrapped around her shoulders, watching embers settle into quieter forms of heat.

There was something she had not said yet.

Not because it was dangerous — but because saying it would

make time visible.

"I know this isn't the end," she said quietly.

Thorne glanced up but didn't interrupt.

"Not of the road," she clarified. "And not of… this."

She gestured broadly — not to him alone, but to the space between them, the way their proximity no longer spiked her awareness or forced restraint. The way *want* existed now without urgency, without triggering consequence or collapse.

Thorne studied her with steady attention. "No," he said. "It isn't."

Astrid exhaled slowly. "I'm aware that what I'm choosing right now is… provisional."

"Yes."

"I'm not denying anything," she continued. "Not desire. Not possibility. I'm pacing."

The word felt precise and dangerous in the best way.

Thorne nodded. "And that's different from fear."

"Yes," she agreed. "Fear rushes toward certainty. Pacing accepts duration."

She stared into the firelight, watching the way flame lengthened and shrank according to fuel rather than command.

"There will come a point," she said slowly, "when choosing not to act will cost more than acting."

Thorne did not contradict her.

"And when that moment arrives," Astrid continued, voice steady but thin, "I want the choice to be conscious. Mine. Not driven by imbalance or necessity or anyone else's expectation."

Thorne shifted closer — not touching, but within intentional distance. "You're saying you're not closing the door."

"No," she said. "I'm making sure it opens when I'm still myself."

Silence followed, dense but clean.

"You should know," Thorne said carefully, "that I'm not interpreting this as delay indefinitely."

Astrid met his gaze. "Good. Because it isn't."

The honesty settled like a stone placed precisely where a foundation needed weight.

"I don't want to rush into the future just because it exists," she said. "And I don't want to pretend I don't see it coming."

Thorne smiled faintly. "That's the most dangerous kind of awareness."

"Yes," she agreed. "But it's also the kind that lasts."

She leaned back, fatigue threading through her now, deep and real. Her body would ask for rest long before her mind did.

That was new too.

"I'm going to need more time," she said — not as apology. As fact.

Thorne's reply came without hesitation. "You have it."

"And you won't disappear while I take it."

"No."

The certainty of that did something sharp and almost painful inside her chest.

"Not because you're waiting?" she pressed. "But because you're choosing to be here."

"Yes," he said simply.

Astrid closed her eyes, breath slowing.

For the first time, she let herself imagine — not specifics, not heat or culmination — but *continuation*. Shared travel. Quiet mornings. Gradual escalation not forced by danger but earned by trust.

Not now.

Later.

And because it was *later*, not *never*, the image did not frighten her.

✦✦✦

They shared the meal after that, ordinary and grounding, the day's fatigue settling into their limbs with familiar honesty. Astrid found herself leaning — not unconsciously, not carefully — into the quiet reality of being accompanied.

Not anchored.

Accompanied.

Some hours later, as stars began to thread their way into the darkening sky, Astrid stood again at the edge of the clearing and placed her palm briefly against the soil.

The land answered — not by acting, not by correcting — but by remembering.

Far beneath her awareness, something adjusted.

Not violently.

Incrementally.

Ancient bindings, tuned too tightly to permanence, felt the pressure of repetition instead. Old protections designed around finished outcomes recalibrated, uncertain how to respond to power that refused to conclude.

In places Astrid would never see, names long trusted to mean *final* became provisional again.

Eyes opened.

Not in alarm.

In assessment.

This time, Astrid sensed it faintly — not as weight, but as distance crossed.

"Book," she murmured to herself, using the temple word for

consequences that hadn't arrived yet.

Thorne glanced at her. "Did the land say something?"

"No," she replied after a moment. "It noticed."

That night, she slept without dreams.

In the deep hours before dawn, when the world belonged neither to day nor night, Astrid woke briefly and found Thorne awake beside her, gaze lifted toward the sky with the relaxed vigilance of someone who had chosen watch rather than been assigned to it.

She turned slightly and rested her hand against his forearm.

He covered it without surprise.

No oath was spoken.

No future promised.

But somewhere far away, something that had depended on endings marked the moment — and understood, finally, that it was dealing not with a solution…

…but with a **continuation**.

And continuations, when chosen consciously, had a habit of becoming trouble.

The good kind.

Back of Book

Daughter of Earth and Fire

by G. J. Stein

Astrid was once a cleric of the Earth—until her magic stopped obeying.

Exiled after a healing spell nearly destroys what it was meant to mend, Astrid is left with power that surges instead of listens, answers instead of heals. Cut off from her temple and her god, she sets out in search of control, guided only by stubborn faith and the rumor of an ancient dragon who judges those bold—or desperate—enough to seek it.

At her side walks Thorne, a half-giant guardian bound by oath and restraint. Quiet, formidable, and relentless in his patience, he offers protection without possession—and becomes the one place Astrid's magic does not spiral out of control. But proximity brings its own danger. Desire sharpens. Choices become heavier. And every step Astrid takes leaves consequences written into the land itself.

To master her power, Astrid must face a truth no blessing can erase: control cannot be forced, restraint cannot be hollow, and power that listens will demand honesty in return. The trial waiting beneath the mountain is not a test of strength—but of what she is willing to refuse.

A slow-burn fantasy romance filled with tension, consent, and dangerously deliberate restraint, *Daughter of Earth and Fire* is the first installment in an epic series where intimacy is earned, power is negotiated, and love is not denied—but carefully, consciously chosen.

About the Author

G. J.Stein writes character-driven fantasy focused on consequence, restraint, and power that must be consciously chosen.

Daughter of Earth and Fire is the first novel set in the world of **Verahald**, where magic listens before it answers and intimacy is earned rather than assumed.

G. J. Stein maintains a clear separation between creative work and professional practice.

You can connect with me on:

https://www.gjsteinbooks.com

Subscribe to my newsletter:

https://sendfox.com/gjsteinbooks

www.ingramcontent.com/pod-product-compliance
Lightning Source LLC
LaVergne TN
LVHW090512110826
845146LV00003B/821

* 9 7 9 8 9 9 5 3 2 9 4 0 4 *